METHALODON

A NOVEL BY

HUGO NAVIKOV

SEVEREDPRESS

METHALODON

Copyright © Severed Press

WWW.SEVEREDPRESS.COM

ISBN: 978-1-922861-80-1

METHALODON

Like smugglers had for centuries, the men spoke in English.

"At zero feet, the fishing is looking clear and fine."

"Aye, copy that," replied Pedro on the luxury fishing vessel which served as the command boat. It was intended to look like three South Americans were just way off course, not accompanying a drug-laden narco-submarine. "Stay this course. The fishermen need their bait."

"Aye, the *bait*. Heh."

They weren't very good at code.

But that didn't matter: El Gato bought this submarine and had the four men trained at great expense so the helicopters and all that Coast Guard hardware couldn't spot them unless they already knew where to look.

And, El Gato assured them, the Americans had no idea where to look anyway. (He was named "El Gato" by his underlings long ago, because he pounced like a cruel cat and he liked to sound like his idol, the Mexican drug lord superstar, El *Chapo*. No one ever doubted the abilities of El Chapo, that was for sure. Not even his late father, who, until his unfortunate chainsaw-related death, was Chapo's main rival.)

The drug-laden, cigar-shaped submarine—a real iron one, not one of those tourist all-plastic-with-big-windows jobs—was supported by a surface vessel that didn't have so much as a joint on board. They were there in case the *federales* tried to espy the sub as it moved up the coast, underwater, from Tijuana to San Diego. The *Floater*, well, floated on the surface directly above the sub, their movements practically synchronized so to make the sub invisible using the authorities' usual detection methods.

As Gato himself didn't accompany the shipments, staying only in radio contact every few minutes because he was a complete control freak, the boat wouldn't have any fugitives from justice on board and wouldn't have any legitimate reason to stop and detain them. To all the world, it looked like a Mexican pleasure sailor was just out sea fishing.

When there were no *gringos* around—the Mexican Maritime Search and Rescue wouldn't waste time hunting smugglers unless the Americans gave them a hugely financially rewarding reason to do so–the sub would rise to just poking its top above the surface, allowing the air exchangers a break. The surface and subsurface vessels zipped along at 10 knots, headed for San Diego by the end of the day. Packed into the sub was more than $20 million in coke, wrapped in secure waterproof packaging just in case the sub started sinking by its own volition, so the coke could be retrieved later if they had to scuttle the ship to keep it from sinking to crush depth and making everything impossible to recover, even in theory. If jettisoned, the coke would sink much more slowly or even slowly start rising to the surface, with just enough air inside the packaging to keep it from going too deep and maybe enough to get it into fishing distance before it could be recovered.

The men were a lot cheaper to replace, so there was really no rush as far as Gato was concerned, as long as they could still make the scheduled drop. It's not like he didn't have two of these small subs. Gato loved them especially because they stood out from anything lesser smugglers used and made him look extra smart and special. He thought of painting them yellow, but thought the risk of being spotted wasn't worth what he thought was a truly hilarious reference. But he didn't feel like it was worth it to kill men just for not appreciating a brilliant joke.

"Big shark coming up, *Buceadora*," Pablo, on the yacht *Flotadora* straight above at the surface, said warily. But he could tell it wasn't just a regular shark, or else he wouldn't have bothered to alert the sub. "Davi, you copy?"

"Is it what I think it is? Please tell me it isn't what I think it is? That it really is just a really big shark, *sí?*" the nominal captain of the sub said with a thin voice. ("Nominal" because Gato got kind of crazy if anyone said *he* wasn't the *jefe* of everything.) The submariners were blind as bats even at the surface unless they had the periscope up, and the periscope wasn't going to show them what was headed their way below the waves.

"*No sé*," Pablo said, forgetting to use his English. "I can't see it, just on the radar it looks like … a really big fish. *Really* big."

"I'm looking, too, hang on," the sub said. And after a moment, incredulously: "*Mierda*. I think it is the Megalodon."

Did he say the Megalodon? As in … *the goddamn MEGALODON?*

"What? A *what?* Davi–I mean *Buceadora*–that's got to be a myth. It was a joke by the scientists."

There was silence on the line, making Pedro gulp audibly. "Really? There's *really* dinosaurs again?"

"For the love of Mother Mary, Roberto–read a news site once in a while. They cloned a male and female and they escaped the facility … how can you not remember this? Now we got these *nojenta* dinosaurs swimming around."

"So they eat ships and stuff? Like, swallow them whole?"

"Negative, *Buceadora*," Pablo said with not a little exasperation. "I mean, *sí*, they *can*, but they get enough fish and surfers and stuff to keep them from getting too hungry, is what I think. Mostly we got to watch out for it trying to mate with you, heh."

"It's getting kind of close." The submariner sounded increasingly nervous. "They *never* eat boats?"

Pablo started to answer, then froze: While it was true that, even with the original mates and now, from what he had read online, half a dozen new monster babies hatched into the environment, none of the giant resurrected dinosaur sharks was recorded as attacking a *boat* … but they swallowed a couple of research vessels whole. Megs didn't usually chew, using their teeth mostly to tear through things as needed to get to their prey they wanted to swallow.

Those tiny research submersibles would be light snacks compared to *Buceadora*, since they weren't iron, they had windows and mostly scientific equipment and weren't made to go very deep. On the other hand, *Buceadora* was made of iron rather than aluminum and had only tiny windows at the waterline when surfaced. But they were almost the exact same size.

But Pablo decided against giving Davi all of that disturbing information that really wouldn't help him if the Meg did feel munchy. So instead he said, "Um … you should head for shallow water. Like, *imediatamente*."

A shriek came from the radio: "*¿¡¿Que?!?*"

"Just to be safe. It looks like it's heading straight for us. Well, *you*. But get going, *amigo*."

Pedro could almost hear the *gulp* on the other end of the radio. "Definitely a Megalodon, though?"

It was most definitely a Megalodon, and it was quite obviously mistaking *Buceadora* for a smaller shark like a Great White or even a whale shark. Much like modern sharks, Megalodons loved to chow down on their smaller cousins. "Just go ahead and max out your speed–get the hell out of here. We'll meet back up later, watch the radio–what– *puta merda!*"

As the monster sped up and shot in a beeline for the sub, Pedro was struck by guilt at how glad he was that he had stayed aboard the boat and not gone down into the sub with Davi. Their radio shut off as the button was released, no doubt because they were hitting the controls to go all out in their getaway from the fifty-foot-long ancient shark as it bore down on them. But Pedro still thought he could hear them screaming as the Meg opened its jaws wide under the water and, in plain sight, sucked in and closed down behind the *Buceadora* without even needing to bite.

All of a sudden Pedro's mind clicked and he screamed, "OH, NO–*THE DRUGS!!!*"

So swiftly he almost rolled himself off the boat, Pedro whipped around and grabbed the harpoon, already loaded with a tracking device in the almost event a load of cocaine fell off the boat (when it was transported like that, which was still the more common mode of smuggling transport than subs) and sank so they could easily find it again and liberate it–and the smugglers themselves–from a watery fate.

He fired almost without thinking or aiming and nailed the Meg right through the couple of feet of water. It would have been hard to miss, but impossible to hit once it got out into open water and dove deep.

The men were as good as dead, Pedro thought, but the coke would be safe inside the iron vessel. And that meant El Gato wouldn't kill him. At least not yet. At least not unless they couldn't somehow get the drugs out of the sub, which right now meant they'd somehow have to get it out of the Megalodon.

Pedro looked at the radio, on which Gato was screaming for an update. He didn't want to answer, but this boat didn't have enough range to get him far enough away, no matter if it was across the entire ocean. And even then, Gato would find him.

It crackled again, and then there was a yelling *grande jefe*: "Pedro! What is happening? Why am I losing contact with the cocaine–I mean, with Davi–on the sub?"

He picked up the VHF transmitter and reluctantly depressed the button. "Sir, *Buceadora* has been lost."

"Lost? *Lost?* What? You had better not be serious, *puta*. Also, if you are making a joke, I will kill you, certainly you realize that, eh?"

"No, *jefe*, the sub has been swallowed by a Megalodon. The dinosaur shark thing, *entende*? I think they might even still be alive in there."

"*Bueno*, Pedro, but … if you don't mind my asking … *where is my GODDAMN COCAINE?*"

"It's inside the sub. Inside the shark. The, um, Megalodon. It should be safe."

"Oh, it should be *safe*, good, good …" El Gato's mock satisfied tone alone made Pedro's anus pucker. "Tell me, *meu bom amigo*, did you ever watch the Shark Week on television?"

"*Sí*, of course." Where was this possibly going?

"Then you know that sharks–and ancient ones, too, I think you can bet your life on that–have the strongest stomach acid in the entire animal kingdom. It can eat through solid iron in a matter of days, did you know that?"

"I did not, *jefe*, no." Wow, El Gato must have *really* been into Shark Week, maybe because he had so much business with the ocean?

"Well, there you go."

"*¿Que?* I don't–"

"No, I mean that literally," Gato interrupted. "There you go … into the goddamn monster. Get in there and get me my cocaine or you'll be, what do they say, *asleep with the pez* yourself."

"*¿Que?* How? I don't–"

"You don't, you *don't*, you *DON'T!* You mean you *won't*, *claro?*" Before Pedro could even sputter anything else, Gato added, "You know what? Forget it. What's the closest island to where you are? I mean–who gives the ass of a rat where *you* are–I mean the giant shark that has my *two tons* of uncut meth and coke."

Pedro checked his chart. The nearest land was a little island he knew was used by both smugglers on one side to hide drugs and by trust fund kids from the mainland on the other to party down using some of the same exact drugs after it was cut and resold and resold again through the system. He had been there before, and a boat full of coke (which he sincerely wished he was on right then instead of following a sea monster around) would have fit right in.

"Persuasion Island. About four hours from here at ten knots."

"I'll be there as soon as I get the pilot sobered up," Gato said. "I want to know exactly where that dirty fish is when my Ferragamos meet the deck. *¿Claro?*"

"*Sí*. I have a tracker on the Meg."

"What the–you *do?* Why the hell didn't you lead with that? I had my hand on the button to blow up your little luxury liner there. *Estúpido*, for real. *Jefe* out."

Pedro's hands were shaking. "Copy that." He paused. Gato was probably bluffing. Probably. "*Estúpido* out."

* * *

Inside the sub looking out, it seemed darker than it ever had before. The windows at the very top, used for looking over the surface in place of the periscope, showed only black. Actually, that wasn't exactly right, Davi noticed as he peered down to see what else was in the stomach of the dinosaur: there was a very faint bioluminescence, as the Megalodon must have swallowed a lot of small creatures as well that glowed in the dark deep underneath the surface.

But that was it. Other than that, it was as pitch as it got. There were strange sounds, some like a human stomach gurgling and groaning, but others like the wooden planks of an enormous, mythical vessel straining and stretching as the waves commanded.

They were alive, him and the weirdly silent Manny; they had food and the sub scrubbed its own air, at least as long as the battery maintained power; and the monster had just gulped them down, not even touching them with those dinner-plate–sized teeth. But … what in the name of *Santa María* were they going to do now except just get digested or whatever by this damned monster?

"Manny."

"*Que.*" Not even a question, like *What?* It was just *What.* The tone of someone who had totally checked out or given up. Or both.

"We're not dead, you know?"

"Thank you for that, *amigo*. But we might as well be, yeah? It's like Jonah and the Whale, but we are not the righteous." He thought for a moment. "Maybe more like Pinocchio without the talking bug."

"Look, man, you seen a lot of movies. So have I. This is like that–all we got to do is make this big *puta* sneeze. Then we shoot out like a ball out of a cannon."

Manny scoffed, not even bothering to look at Davi. "Yeah? What are you gonna do, find a giant feather to tickle his nose with?"

"No, not a feather, *idiota*," Davi said, and opened the locked hold. He pulled out a two-kilo package of pure factory-made methamphetamine and held it for Manny to get his stupid head around. "Two kilos of this is enough to kill an elephant–you bet your ass it's enough to make this big *bastardo* sneeze or throw up or *something*. To do something to relieve the itch, which has got to include getting us the hell out of its system, yeah?"

Manny sat up, his eyes alight. "Holy shit, man … we got this!"

We, huh? Davi thought, definitely unkindly. *You didn't do nothing, you lump.* "Prepare the chamber. Do something around here for once."

Manny got up and emptied the decompression chamber they used when they needed to do an EV to hide more coke or do maintenance when the water wasn't too deep and the pressure too high. Then Davi used his pocket knife to cut the packaging open, and there it was: pure crystal methamphetamine, the young people's new favorite. (There had been more than a few deliveries of coke to the rich kids on Persuasion Island, but of course never with the sub—meth was more exotic and even attractively dangerous in *ojos de los jóvenes idiotas.*)

"You want?" Davi said, indicating the drugs. He most certainly himself did *not* do any kind of stuff when he was inside that tin can, whether it was meth or the big packages in more ways than one, the cocaine.

"Gimme."

"Suit yourself. I ain't having it in this small space–I guarantee I will *freak out*," Davi said with a laugh.

He watched Manny take and use his knife to lift a frickin' sand dune of meth up to his nose and snorted the whole thing in like it was a Pixy Stix full of colored sugar. Then Davi took the rest of the opened package and dumped it into the chamber, then swung the hatch shut.

"Fill it," he said to Manny, whose response was an "aye" made extremely ragged because of the magnificent shock obviously traveling like lightning through his system. They watched as the water filled the chamber and the meth swirled up and out into the water-filled stomach of the Megalodon.

"Filled," Manny said, sneezed hard, and fell unconscious to the floor as if he was dead. Which he wasn't, based on the twitching, but it definitely looked like there was going to be nobody home for a while.

Davi stared at the fresh body of his co-mariner and thought two things, neither of which he was particularly proud of, but whatever. The first was: *Hey, more oxygen for me!*

And the second: *This shit is strong*. He hoped the Meg would sneeze or throw up from the irritation or whatever. If he needed to throw out more meth or even start in on the coke, he would, Gato be damned. He had to get out of this Jurassic Park knockoff-ass movie … even if it cost him his thumbs.

There was a low rumble in the monster that Davi could feel deep inside the thing's stomach. Suddenly there was a whoosh of water flowing the other way from how the stuff had come into the stomach, including the sub, into the esophagus or whatever. This must have been the vomiting.

It was starting. Soon the Meg would expel enough meth to kill a football team, and Davi felt actual hope the sub would go out with it. Sure, any barracuda or sharks or whatever would quickly suck the mania-producing drug into their systems, but the sub couldn't be *swallowed* by those things. It was a good tradeoff.

* * *

"I can't believe *Chris Newman* is our fishing guide," the college kid said, and this one was still relatively sober. That shouldn't have been very surprising given they were less than two hours into the excursion, but his six vacation-mates were either already as far gone as the sleaziest smack addict on Skid Row or as drunk as …

… well, as drunk as Chris whenever he wasn't at the controls of the *Killer Whale*. "Yeah, glad to be a story for when you get home," he said. "Maybe along with the swordfish you have to spend two thousand bucks to get stuffed and shipped back."

The kid, his name was Jamie Cant as Chris remembered, missed his tone entirely. "You really think we'll catch a swordfish? Holy crap. Or *carp*, right?" He laughed and laughed, wheezing until he had to rush over to the side and puke into the water.

Maybe he hadn't been as sober as Chris had thought. But then, why would be be? These rich kids came to Persuasion Island, so named because explorers who found the four-square mile-island on their way to South America stopped there as a Persuasion. They loaded up with breadfruit and turtles and fresh water just in case the longitude issue created a problem. Also, the island being just south of the equator meant the sailors could have ended up stuck in the doldrums for weeks, where the wind blew every which way, if it blew at all.

And Persuasion Island did blow, Chris thought. Nothing but asshole trust-fund college students taking advantage of booze and coke and even sometimes meth that their goddamn adult vacation guides provided them–ironic, maybe, since drugs had been dumped or stashed there for decades as a Persuasion (hence the name, although its official moniker was something French), the drugs were often dug up later by the kids or the couple of hundred locals themselves in order to support the *louche* lifestyle Chris himself had come there for.

Jamie's pals, whom Chris had christened Barf and Puke–there were identical nicknames given during almost every trip, sadly–now nearly screamed with excitement at the two deep-sea fishing stations at the aft of the boat. They were trying to control the poles bolted to oarlocks so they couldn't be lost overboard (there were plenty below decks just in case) and the poles were actually jerking like something had been caught. Usually Chris was the only one able to catch something and reel it in (he did it like it was the rich kid himself doing it), but this time it seems that the bait had actually been taken by something big.

"Chris! *Newman! Get your sad ass back here!*"

Oh, how he loved these spoiled assholes treating him like the hired help.

Which, of course, he was. But he still didn't like it.

"Hey, looks like you hooked a big one, Barf–I mean, my man," Chris said with feigned enthusiasm, choosing to concentrate on the money he got for putting up with them while he went deep-sea fishing, not the worst of working conditions, to be honest. "You're gonna have to haul this one in. You can do it!"

And the kid very likely could do it, with his gym muscles and all. Yes, he might have to wrestle at the oarlock a bit, but it was well bolted to the–

There was an ungodly creak at the aft, and Chris got there just in time to see the oarlocks buckle and rip off its bolts, taking a chunk of the aft beam with it. Not to mention the five-hundred–dollar rod and reel.

Holy Jesus, Chris's mind shouted at him. In thirty years of ocean fishing, he had never seen this. And it was going to be expensive as hell to fix.

Puke, standing next to Barf in the eastern Pacific sun, was pissed. "Thanks for taking your time, asshole."

Barf had unbuckled himself from the chair that kept the *Killer Whale*'s fishermen from being yanked out to sea by a whale shark or giant tuna, and was now just staring out at the dark water where his prize catch had disappeared with what had been in his hands just a moment before. "Yeah," he said, his earlier intoxicated jubilation gone. "We're paying top goddamn dollar for this, and your cheap garbage just *busted?*"

"It's … it's never happened before," Chris said, himself staring at the chunk of the back of the boat gone and the water where it went. "You must have hooked onto a whale shark or something. You wouldn't have been able to reel than in anyway, Hoss. Good thing you were buckled in or it would've yanked you over the side."

"I'm calling my father," Puke said, and started thumbing at the phone that was already in his hand to take video of Barf's amazing catch. In a moment, though, he stopped, frustration at being kneecapped on his sunburned face. "No signal out here."

Barf laughed derisively. "Yeah? Out here in the middle of the ocean? That's why they use *radios*, dumbass."

Puke raised his chin and sniffed like he was a lord dismissing a servant and said to Chris, "I need to use the radio."

"Is your father within earshot of a nautical radio right now?"

Barf laughed. Puke steamed. "Fine, asshole. But now I'm a *survivor*, you get that? When we get to shore, I'm gonna lawyer up and–*GAHHH!!!*"

"*JESUS CHRIST!*" Barf shouted as a full-size swordfish–five hundred pounds at least, Chris's brain automatically calculated–leapt out of the water, speared Puke through the chest, and fell back into the ocean with the college kid skewered like a shish kabob, screaming all the way down.

Chris's instincts kicked in–there would be time for horror later–and he pointed hard toward the hatch in the deck. He bellowed at the six other young people standing and staring in utter shock, "Below! Everyone down below!" They didn't move, frozen in place. "*NOW!*"

His command finally reached their brains and they almost fell over each other getting to the hatch and down the ladder to the below decks.

Blood from the sudden violation of Puke's bodily envelope (the coroner's report was already in his head, although there would never be one the way the kid was taken back into the deep to be consumed by the many, many predators) was splattered all over the deck, so Chris had to be extremely careful making his way on the deck to–

"*HOLY–*" Chris cried out as a shark, a goddamn full-size bull shark, flung itself out of the water and all the way onto the boat's deck, its fifteen feet of solid ocean muscle thrashing and his huge mouth full of razor-sharp teeth snapping.

Chris fell back and almost hurled himself down the hatch after the college kids. When he got there, he saw these "no homo" frat boys holding one another in shock and fear.

"What is this? *What's happening?!?*"

Listening to the shark expending itself above them, Chris said weakly, "I don't know."

***

Abbie Marnoch scanned the sonar aboard the research submersible *Sinker*, which was mostly windows but that didn't help much in the very low light of this depth. There was a huge shape on the sonar, which had to be the Meg. He didn't know where the mate was, although they were most often pretty close to each other. He'd just have to keep an eye out–he didn't want to be a swallowed lunch, and so kept one hand near the only defense he had, the equivalent of an underwater stink bomb that would repel any creature from eating his little craft.

"Anything, Marnoch?" came from Andrzej on the longwave radio. He was aboard their surface vessel, the *Participant*, which carried the scientists and mariners supporting the research expedition.

"No, but it's got to be near here. That little island attracts fish, and fish attract the Meg."

"Thanks for the lesson, boss."

"Sorry, sorry, just a habit," he said, and it was: He was used to being around people who just feared the existence of a Megalodon on the loose–two of them–due largely to negative media coverage that made the whole thing sound like *Jaws*. The Meg was actually quite peaceful unless it was provoked in some way, since really it had no competition for food in modern times. Maybe when it was in its original habitat millions of years ago, but now there were no other mega-predators, just sharks that it swallowed if it needed to.

No, they had found that, absent some kind of agitation, the Meg didn't really bother anyone except for swallowing, say, the occasional research submersible that it swallowed thinking it was food. Of course, before it had eaten through the protective iron netting at the research station where researchers *way* overstepped ethical boundaries by cloning the dinosaur fish from ancient DNA, they found that agitation, like that from eating a venomous fish, made it almost blindly angry and it would eat and rip apart anything in its path.

In fact, that's how the two Megs had escaped where they were cloned in the first place.

However, it was that very escape and complete impossibility of catching such huge carnivorous creatures that allowed greater research opportunities, and Marnoch had been able to get near it several times–*always* from the back, *always* from behind–to study how it behaved in the open water.

This excursion was to see if the monstrous shark-like creatures had mated and laid eggs, or even to catch sight of the offspring. There couldn't be any predators for the Megs to fear, as they were many times the size of even the biggest modern shark. So their making more Megalodons could pose an issue to the shipping and fishing industries, something Marnoch was keenly aware of in his mission to protect and learn about them.

In the final analysis, he believed that Megs were mostly harmless except to those creatures they sucked in or the particular, unlucky ships they decided to chomp on for whatever reason. No, lacking any kind of other sea life that could pose a threat, the Meg was very unlikely to get agitated or stressed. If that did happen, it would be a feeding frenzy unlike anything any ichthyologist had ever seen.

"There's a boat out there," Andrzej radioed down to the *Sinker*.

"Above the Meg?"

"Negative–sonar shows our friend a mile east of the seacraft, which is a quarter mile from us. But …" Andrzej hesitated here, which sent a chill down Marnoch's spine. "There's some kind of … *cloud* right underneath the seacraft."

"A cloud? That must be multiple creatures, maybe a large school?"

Andrzej blew out a breath. "Could be, I guess. Permission to approach and hail?"

"Yes," Marnoch said. "Aye." The nautical lingo still escaped him. He spent a good amount of time on these ships, but he was never part of the mariner component, so he frequently forgot to use the seafaring words. It was kind of distracting from his main work, but he wanted to be respectful.

"*My God,*" Andrzej said with awe in his voice. "Marnoch, we have to get in closer."

"What? Why?" He could now see the cloud more clearly on the sonar, and it was just as he had thought … as far as it was a collection of sea life. He had said a school, but this wasn't that at all. All the fish were different, or at least there was every size and shape of fish thrashing around under the boat, beside the boat, and, holy crap, even–

"They're jumping onto that boat! *Onto the goddamn boat!*"

Marnoch could hardly process what was happening, but he started surfacing. Swordfish could leap out of the water, but, contrary to *Jaws 2*, sharks did not jump. Barracuda could not jump.

And these things were *jumping* out of the water.

"*Mayday, mayday, mayday!*" came the cry from the VHF onboard radio. "*This is the* Killer Whale*, call number NY 1975 SP! My position–*"

"Roger, roger, *Killer Whale*, we see you," Andrzej responded on the ship's radio, and Marnoch was near enough to the surface now to pick up shipboard communications. "What is happening?"

"This is Captain Chris Newman. I have seven passengers here, we are below decks. I don't know what's happening, but the ship is being attacked by … um … *multiple fish*. One casualty from animal attack. We are–*oh my God*–" A fearful rending sound came over the radio before the mic was cut.

"*Killer Whale*? *Killer Whale,* respond. Captain Newman, please respond!" Marnoch could hear Andrzej clicking the transmitter button again and again, and repeating the call for the ship to respond. Then the Polish captain radioed Marnoch, shouting "Marnoch, the boat's coming apart. Can you see?"

The submersible had surfaced now, and when he opened the hatch, indeed he could see that the *Killer Whale* was going down. The hull was coming apart as well, and Marnoch could hear a multitude of male voices yelling for help.

"Can we help them?" Andrzej radioed as the crew started bringing up the *Sinker*.

"The *Participant* has a steel hull, right?"

"Damn right."

"Then they can't get at us." He paused. "At least, I don't think they can. Now get my butt on board and let's do it."

***

Chris didn't scream with the rest of them five minutes later when the hull began cracking under the assault of sharks, dolphins, swordfish, and God knew what other large predators in the eastern Pacific as they rammed the composite fiber-reinforced plastic that made up most of the *Killer Whale* again and again.

What in the holy hell was happening? Everything had gone insane. The fish, mammals, whatever it was that sharks were–*everything* was thrashing around, slamming into the boat intentionally or accidentally, and now the hull cracked once, then twice–

–and then the salt water started rushing in.

They were trapped in the area below decks, water rapidly filling the hold. More screams, more faces looking at him, the captain, and beseeching him to do something, as if he weren't trapped down there as much as they were.

Then the hull broke in half, a crack spreading up the side, then the brackish water rushed over them and washed them all from the hold like they were inside a pot being rinsed out. In the bubble-filled melee, Chris could open his eyes only for a second, but that was enough to see one good thing and one extremely bad thing.

The good thing was that he was just a couple of feet below the surface, as he could see the blue sky above; but the bad thing was that there was blood mixed in with the bubbles. Blood meant that one of the dumbass kids had been bitten, possibly ripped apart, definitely dead or about to be dead, surrounded by sharks and other sharp-toothed fish as all of them were.

It would be a matter of seconds before these things–the area was full of Great Whites, who usually minded their own business around boats, but with this shit, who knew?–sensed the blood and went into a feeding frenzy. They were all as good as dead.

An air horn sounded from the surface, making Chris jump even though he was underwater. He could open his eyes only for a second with the salt stinging them immediately, but what he did see was a shadow at the surface …

It was a boat. And it was signaling them with the air horn, knowing that sound travels through water faster and more strongly than through air, so it was the perfect way to attract their attention with the radio now floating, or sinking, with the rest of the *Killer Whale*.

He opened his eyes for a moment again. He could see that the kids who weren't already bobbing at the surface–they weren't *kids* kids, but they sure acted like it–must have opened their eyes long enough to look up at where the air horn had come from and were already swimming toward the surface, toward their rescuers–

A garbled scream came from nearby, though Chris–already making his way as fast as he could to where the boat was–couldn't pinpoint the direction amidst all the auditory chaos. But he knew what it was.

The sharks. The barracuda. Jellyfish, who knew what. They were now attacking in whatever frenzy had made them destroy his boat in the first place. The screams were limited to one per person, as no one could inhale any air to let out a second. And besides, screaming doesn't last long when you're bitten in half by a bull shark or your throat is ripped out by a barracuda at full speed.

His heart told him to stop swimming up and start swimming down to save–or at least help–the passengers he was responsible for, but his brain told him to get to the air and, God willing, into that boat that the frenzied creatures hadn't been able to take down.

OH SHIT THE MEG

is what his mind suddenly shouted louder than the air horn.

The Megalodon could easily rise and snatch this boat–which was bigger than the *Killer Whale* by a long shot–in its jaws and crunch it and swallow it in less time than it would take Chris to crunch and swallow a bag of peanut M&Ms poured directly into his mouth.

How fast could a Meg swim? It was at least a mile off, and Jesus, it was giant. He had seen one once not too long after they escaped from where they had been created from old DNA or however the hell they made the things. He really never cared to see one again, especially now. He didn't care that they usually didn't bother surface ships–they *usually* didn't bother them, unless they felt agitated for some reason. "Usually" wasn't good enough.

He reached the surface and filled his lungs with sweet, sweet oxygen, all brought inside him with a gasp like none he had ever had before.

The boat was right there, and in seconds a life preserver splatted into the water next to him. As he grabbed it and was pulled toward the ladder on the side of the vessel, he looked back at the debris that was once his beloved *Killer Whale*.

Yet that wasn't even what struck him and made him want to scream.

No, what made him almost want to throw himself back into the water and save them was the passengers–half a dozen young men who had trusted him to keep them safe while they were having the fishing trip of their lives–thrashing and screaming as they were torn apart by bull sharks, tiger sharks, goddamn barracuda, and things he couldn't place. But all of the predators leaped–practically in some cases, literally in others–from the water in fury as they reduced the kids to pieces and then ravenously devoured those pieces.

Chris was the last person to be hauled aboard whatever kind of weird boat this was. There was no one left in the water who wasn't dead or less than sixty seconds from death.

"*Move! Move now!*" the bearded man shouted at the crew of the vessel as he helped Chris get on board. "*It's coming!*"

Oh, hell. Chris knew what "it" meant. The Meg was on its way.

On the deck now with a huge towel thrown around him, he saw that one of the kids had made it out of the water. Just *one*. Shaking with fear and relief and sadness, Chris went to him and, without a word, opened his arms to give him an embrace.

And the kid–Jamie was his name, Chris remembered now–hauled off and punched him right in the face.

*****

Marnoch could now see the Meg, a dark shadow under the surface. It was getting nearer every moment, and although the steel hull of the *Participant* protected them from any sharks or orca of any size now, the Megalodon's jaws could crush them like the ship was made of papier maché. He wrapped the man–holy crap, it was Chris "The Fishing Guy" Newman!–in a towel and practically leaped towards the bridge.

Megs traveled as fast as sixteen knots. The *Participant* could reach twenty-three.

"Haul ass!" Marnoch shouted at the boat's captain, Andrzej, who threw the throttle so fast the boat lurched in the water. Marnoch could see that Andrzej knew what was happening with the Meg and was just about to go full speed ahead without Marnoch's command.

(Technically, Marnoch was under Andrzej as far as the *Participant* was concerned, but in practice it was Marnoch's vessel when necessary. This was the first time it had ever been necessary. Andrzej was a *mensch* for being cool with it.)

"Can we outrun it?" Marnoch asked when he finally crossed the twenty feet to where Andrzej stood at the helm. "Can't we go faster and get to the mainland?"

"If we had unlimited fuel, sure. But Marnoch, we've been out here for *days*. We were about to head back to the mainland, when we just got irresistible conditions to make another dive. We have a little in reserve past that, but the engine won't take going full speed for two days. We need to get to shallow water, then the Meg can't get us. Too goddamn huge."

Marnoch knew this, of course, but there was something he didn't know, as he wasn't a navigator: "Is there somewhere nearby we can get into the shallows?"

Andrzej checked the chart on his iPad. "We have Persuasion Island, three hours from here at twenty knots. They must have a marina deep enough for us but too shallow for the Meg."

"Persuasion, Persuasion …" Marnoch thought for a moment, and then it hit him. "Oh, hell–is that the party island?"

"Aye. I bet that's where the boat came from, judging by the 'grizzled' captain and surviving Gen Z'er there on the deck."

"Did you radio in the wreck?"

"Aye. The American Coast Guard *might* be on the way, but the Mexicans only operate within fifty miles of the border. We're kind of on our own here."

Hell and damnation. "Well, I'm going to talk to Chris and find out what the hell happened. Maybe he knows. Probably not, but worth a shot."

Andrzej said with real excitement, "Chris? Is that *Chris Newman?* I watched his show for *years*. This is incredible." He then seemed to remember that lives had been lost and added soberly, "But this is a hell of a way to meet him."

"Plenty of time for hero worship later, Cap. Head for Persuasion."

"Aye, sir." the captain replied, and Marnoch thought again that he was lucky indeed to have a man like Andrzej as his mariner.

As soon as they hit the gas, they could see a lighter, smaller shape in front of the Meg. Jesus Christ, it was a goddamn Great White shark, as long as a Cadillac and twice as impressive. It was churning the water as it swam, seemingly in the throes of whatever had made the other fish insane. But it was far larger, and the effect seemed to be less than that on the smaller predators. But it was still plenty crazed, and–

"What the hell?" Marnoch blurted as he saw …

… as he saw the Meg bite the Great White in half from behind, then opened its maw and sucked in the front end of the (formerly) apex predator like it was a stray egg noodle.

"Forget twenty knots, Captain." He could feel himself slipping into almost a dream state, so mesmerized was he at the carnage that had just happened right before his eyes. "Full speed ahead. Even if the engine goes, there's still a better chance than if that thing catches up with us."

***

Before he had invested in two submarines for smuggling his precious coke and meth, El Gato had purchased a "surplus" Mexican army helicopter. He loved the damned thing, and he wouldn't go down in the sub for any amount of money, seriously. He wasn't claustrophobic as such, but being under the water trapped in a little tube of metal … *no gracias*.

The 'copter could zoom at over one hundred miles per hour, and that's what his pilot, Ebrio, was hitting without too much of a sweat. It had taken a precious hour to get the *bastardo* out of his drunken haze, slapping him around a bit to sober him up, and even that took some time. So they had to go full-bore to the island–they could cover the 350 miles from Gato's home base in Tijuana to the tiny island, so less than four hours–to slap Pedro around and somehow get him down to the sub.

To that end, Gato was sending his smaller narco sub, the *Segunda*, to change tacks and head for the island. They were about 60 miles away from the island Gato knew so well, so about three hours at full speed. And this one had torpedoes.

Well, one torpedo, anyway, and they'd never used it or even done any work on maintenance on it … it was really more something to brag about and make Jalisco green with envy, eh?

But yeah, baby. A *torpedo*.

And a literal ton of cocaine as well. The *Segunda* had been headed for San Diego so packed with coke and meth that it could hold only one crew member, and that submariner, Estaban, had to be pretty much immune to claustrophobia. But landing at Persuasion Island–well, submarines didn't *land*, but whatever–would allow them to unload the shipment into the usual secret holds on the island. The nice thing about Persuasion was that it was three hundred or so miles from the California coast in international waters, so the Americans (or anybody else) didn't have jurisdiction to search the island for the drugs or to seize them even if they could find them.

A long smuggler's tunnel going into the island's rock had been dug by Gato's father (well, by his underlings and their forcible labor) years before, and Gato had made the most of it, posting two guards with AR-47 assault rifles at all times. Occasionally one of the partying American morons would wander near the camouflaged mouth of the tunnel, but in those cases, the guards stayed out of sight. The wealthy *imbéciles* would never find it since they were just drunkenly wandering across the beach, and killing or kidnapping them would just immediately bring the attention of the American Coast Guard, Navy, and *dios* knew what else to the island.

And, as an internationally wanted drug kingpin, that attention was the last thing he wanted.

A voice crackled over the radio. "*Jefe*," Pedro called, "*Jefe*, please respond."

Gato had one question for the *capitán* of the *Flotadora*: "Can you see the monster?"

"Aye, *jefe*. But it is heading toward another boat, one with a little sub on its deck. Should I hold back or continue staying with *el dinosaurio*?"

Goddammit. "Hold back, Pedro. Maybe the animal will make that ship into a snack."

"Gato, there is one thing you should know before you get here."

"*Santa María*, what?"

"The sharks and fish are acting … strange." Gato could hear Pedro gulp–the man had the loudest gulp he had ever heard–and then Pedro added, "Like they are on drugs."

You have got to be kidding me, Gato thought, but people, let alone underlings, rarely tried to joke with him. That would mean they didn't respect him. Nobody joked around his father, that was for sure. He wanted that kind of respect. No–*demanded it*.

Pedro continued, "They, em … the sharks took down a fishing boat just half a mile from where I was. Just rammed it and bit it and made a breach in the hull. The things were almost, like, *flying*."

Gato let out a curse so vile that he almost disgusted himself, then got it together enough to say calmly, "They got into the cocaine. Or the meth. Both, maybe."

"No way, *jefe*," Pedro said, and Gato let this attempt at contradiction slide under the circumstances. "How could they? There's no cocaine or nothing in the water, only on the *Buceadora*, and that's been eaten by the monster."

"No, *cabrón*. It got swallowed, *correcto*? It's an iron-hulled submarine–I guarantee you, it's just sitting inside that thing. Our friends could even still be alive."

"So why are the sharks and fish and things acting so crazy? I've never seen anything breach a polyethylene ... hull ..." Pedro trailed off.

"*Flotadora?* Pedro? What's going on?"

"My apologies, Gato. It's just ... my boat has such a hull."

"You have any fishes bothering you? It sounds like they all went home to sleep it off."

"Sleep? I know you make a joke, *jefe*, but how would these things get cocaine if it's all in the sub?"

"Hell if I know. But I want you to stay close to the thing."

"What if it tries to eat us? Or those coke sharks come back?"

"What do you mean, *what if?* You die, that's *what if*. But guess what, Pedro?"

Another audible gulp from the ship's captain and then, weakly, "*Jefe?*"

"You lose that thing, you're going to die anyway."

***

"*It worked*," Davi said inside the sub, speaking the words almost exactly when he thought them. "The *bastardo* sneezed or coughed or whatever. We can do it, *hermano!*"

But in the strange darkness inside the stomach of the Megalodon, Davi noticed Manny was not just quiet, but lost in his own world, shaking and twitching a little bit. He wasn't full-out freaking or tweaking yet, and maybe he wouldn't. Maybe one big snort wouldn't do him in.

"Hey, *amigo*, we're gonna be okay."

No response from Manny. Was he rocking back and forth? *Jesuchristo*.

"Come on, man. We did it! All we need to do is make it throw up the contents of his stomach. That means us and all these dead sharks and whatever these bones might have been." Despite his positive words, Davi had noticed in the dim, sporadic light outside that some pretty good-sized sharks had come in alive, then died, and now were being dissolved in the acid inside the thing's stomach. That was some strong shit. "We should probably do it sooner than later."

Manny moved his glassy gaze from the bulkhead to Davi's face. His throat was dry and creaky as he said, "And h-how do we do that? All that meth and it just *sneezed*."

Davi almost jumped at Manny's question. "There's more than a ton of pure cocaine on board. If that doesn't make a monster sick, even one this goddamn big, then nothing will. It'll work, my man."

He could see Manny's eyes shift to the neatly packed parcels of coke. Weighing the options. It looked like hope was replacing despair in his whole demeanor.

There wasn't nearly as much meth on the sub, and they hadn't even jettisoned it all into the thing yet. They had knives and cutters and they had a decompression chamber and package after thick package of drugs. And the air would continue to go through the scrubbers as long as they had power.

They could make it. That is, unless the thing's stomach acid–which burned up those sharks in ten minutes or less–was going to eat through the sub's hull.

"Let's get cutting," Davi said. "If this thing don't sneeze us out in two hours, we're dumping this shit right into this son of a *puta*. Nothing alive can take that and not go nuts and puke and die."

"I hope it don't die *before* it throws us up, *amigo*."

"I hope we don't have to dump it and get our *cojones* fed to a different fish when we get out of here. But we got to do what we got to do."

***

The fish had stopped going crazy, Marnoch saw. Whatever had sent them into their . murderous frenzy–enough to take down a good-sized fishing boat–seemed to have abated.

"Looks like we're out of the woods. Or water. What do you think, Mister Newman?"

"For God's sake, call me Chris. I'm not a celebrity anymore."

Marnoch gave a little laugh. "Okay, copy that," he said, and was glad the ocean sun had dried him and the young man who had survived along with him. "But we do need your skills right now."

"How's that?"

Andrzej at the helm was pushing the *Participant* hell bent for leather, and the Meg was falling further and further behind as they sailed toward the island. It, too, seemed less feverish in its pursuit of the boat. Marnoch thought whatever had caused the insanity of the sharks and fish must have something to do with the Meg, but he couldn't imagine what that could be.

It was ironic: He had been searching for the Megalodon to study it and learn more about its habits and ways, and now he was running away from it as quickly as possible. Although these new creatures didn't seem to have a lot of interest in surface vessels, this was no time to test that theory. Or maybe it was the perfect time to test it, but hell if Marnoch was going to have anyone aboard when he did it.

"Marnoch?"

He snapped out of his reverie. "Yeah, sorry. Anyway, we need you to get us a fish."

"Um ... okay."

"As soon as the Meg loses interest in us–it looks like that's starting to happen now–we need to circle back and get one of those sharks or a barracuda or a man-of-war or anything in that hotspot."

"I know I just met you, but with all due respect for your bona fides, that seems completely freaking insane. Why, for God's sake?"

"We need to know what happened, why these creatures decided to attack a *boat*. Outside of *Jaws*, that's almost unheard of."

Chris just wanted to get back to the island, where booze and a bed awaited. There would be the authorities to contact, but some of the trip organizers to the island would be responsible for that; and, obviously, he would have to get a new boat in order to continue his livelihood, but one of the extremely rich kids could help with that. Many of them expressed the desire to be on the crew for their stay on Persuasion Island, and Chris *knew* that one of their daddies would come up with the cash, the cost of which wasn't much more than a rounding error to them. It might even be a nicer vessel … maybe one with a steel hull. No, belay that–*definitely* with a steel hull.

"We have deep-sea fishing equipment on board," Marnoch said to Chris, and then shouted to Andrejz, "How's the Meg?"

"She changed course and now is headed away from us," Andrzej said with relief.

"All right, then, make a heading back to the debris field, please."

There was a significant pause at the helm. Then the mariner said, "Sorry, what did you say?"

"Just what you think I said, man."

"*I'm* the captain of this boat."

"I know, and I respect that," Marnoch said, and stopped there.

Another pregnant pause from Andrzej. Finally, he said with an almost tangible sigh, "Aye, making course for the crazy-shark–infested, dangerous-debris–filled danger zone of death."

"Thank you. We're safe here. Chris Newman is gonna catch us a fish."

"Not hungry at the moment."

Marnoch rolled his eyes, then turned to Chris. "We have oarlocks at the aft gunwale. Let's get the gear and get fishing."

***

Chris saw that Marnoch's research boat must have been well funded, because it had everything a deep-sea fisherman could want, the centerpiece being the Daiwa Dendoh Marine Power Fishing Reel with Deep Sea Power Assist, which ran as much as $4,600 and would allow him to reel in a frickin' *shark* without breaking a sweat. Even on his television show, he had never used such a magnificent rod and reel.

They loaded the system into the oarlocks and Chris took his seat and buckled himself in. It wasn't quite that he wouldn't break a sweat, actually, but the Deep Sea Power Assist was definitely going to make it much easier to bring in one of the big boys.

Marnoch went towards the bow and came back a moment later with the high-end rod and reel, placed them in the oarlocks, then went back and brought a lovely bucket of chum.

"Why aren't you having one of the crew do this?"

He placed the bucket down and fixed Chris with an intense look. "This part isn't research because it's about the other sharks and fish–not the Meg–so my guys can't do it, and it doesn't fall in any of their wheelhouses anyway. It's just not part of their job duties. This is all me–and you, thank God–until we figure out what's going on. I've got to cut the flesh off one of them and analyze it."

"Gotcha." It wasn't that he wasn't excited at using one of the world's most expensive rigs to do some shark fishing, he just didn't totally get why they weren't heading back to the island instead of turning away to do this if it wasn't even part of the research vessel's mission. But he knew well the obsessive nature of guys like Abbie Marnoch–the sea did strange things to people, himself included.

Strange, but not usually as strange as what was happening with these freaking-out fish. "In other words, it's not their fight. I'm the one who has to take the sample and run some tests on it in my little lab below decks."

"No, I get it," Chris said, almost licking his lips at the rod in his hand. Lord, the movement was as smooth as twenty-year-old Scotch. "Well, let's get this party started."

It took a few minutes before Chris noticed they were moving through the flotsam that just a few minutes earlier had been his beloved *Killer Whale*. They were there.

Marnoch dug into the reeking slop bucket of chum with a huge flour scoop and let the blood and guts slide with a sickening *plop* into the water. But then there was a thump at starboard, a deeper thump than the sharp sound of a piece of the *Killer Whale*'s hull. If he hadn't been strapped to the seat, he would have jumped to the side, which is what Marnoch did now.

All the color drained out of Marnoch's face, and he looked almost green.

"What?"

"We … we, um, don't need to drop any more chum."

Chris started to ask why Marnoch would say such a thing, but then a thought came to him that almost made him turn green as well. "It's one of the bodies, isn't it? One of my passengers."

Marnoch swallowed and said, "Part of one."

Christ. "Then where are the sh–"

He was cut off by a Great White–a *Great White*– practically flying out of the water, its tail curling toward its mouth to produce angular momentum that kept it in flight, and hurled itself onto the side of the boat, half in and half out, crushing the starboard beam under its immense weight as it writhed in pain and fury to loose itself or kill everything within chomping distance, or both. The *Participant* groaned at the unbalanced weight and Chris found himself at almost a 30-degree angle as the weight of the massive predator pulled the starboard side of the boat towards the water and a third of the hull on the port side.

"*Watch out!*" Marnoch shouted as one of the crewmen slid on the canted deck right towards the front of the enormous shark–the mouth side, which was the one pointed inward–and into the biting radius of the thing. The shark, gasping for oxygen to run through its gills and practically insane with rage, immediately chomped down and relieved Ferrell of both the top third of his body and his life.

Blood splashed in a wide sheet onto the deck from the remainder of Ferrell's body as it flopped over the side like a sodden sandbag.

The crew, hardened men of the sea and a couple of researchers who had seen plenty of things happen in the ocean, shouted in shock almost as one. They instinctively grabbed harpoons, spears, and other defensive accouterments and ran toward the shark, but to a man stopped when they got even a couple of steps closer and realized how truly humongous the thing was, and that its eyes were rolled up in a last-ditch feeding frenzy, but without any other sliding crew members to munch on in its few remaining moments alive.

"Hold on! *Hold on!*" Marnoch shouted as he scampered across the inclined deck, "Don't do anything!"

But no one was doing anything. The shark was bucking and thrashing, and everyone knew that getting anywhere near it would mean dismemberment quickly followed by death and probably nothing they could do would get the damned shark off the starboard beam anyway. Everyone just stood their ground and waited for either Marnoch or Andrzej to tell them what to do.

But Marnoch didn't give any instructions except, "We can't do anything until it's dead. Just ten or fifteen minutes should do it. Then I can take what I need," and Andrzej looked too traumatized to say a word.

Chris felt a little abashed for thinking *I guess no fishing now?* But the bearded researcher was right– the catch had come to them. He could still throw the line into the water and try to snare something, but no bait was going to outdo a human body–or part of one–streaming blood and guts in a greasy pool in the water.

The Great White thrashed less and less over the next few minutes, but nobody wanted to be the first to get close, no matter how still the shark had become.

Fifteen minutes passed, and that's when Marnoch stepped forward with an enormous serrated fishing knife and cut out a fist-sized cube of flesh from the animal. There was plenty more blood that poured onto the deck, but Chris guessed it must have been important enough to create such a mess.

He could see now that the midsection of the Great White had been cut through by the starboard beam and was dropping blood and chunks of innards into the water below as well as on the deck. Chris thought it would be a gift to the boat's crew if there could be a nice downpour right about then.

Marnoch motioned for him and the two other researchers, one with a golden yellow beard and one with a black one to Marnoch's brown, to come below. Chris wasn't quite sure why he was being invited, but he was very glad to be going where he couldn't see the massive dead shark over the side of the boat.

The *Participant* was still listing to starboard at an alarming angle, but it didn't seem as though the boat was going to capsize or have that section of the steel hull give way. They would have to find a way to get the thing off the beam or they weren't going anywhere, but this wasn't his tub and so that wasn't his job. Not yet, anyway. He was probably the most experienced mariner on the boat, everyone else being at least twenty years younger than his fifty-four years, and if he had to be the one to use the winches or other equipment to remove the thing, then so be it.

Chris followed the yellow and brown beards down the ladder and then to the small lab all the way aft. There were various instruments the function of which Chris couldn't even begin to guess.

But all Marnoch did was sit in the chair bolted to the floor and place the still-glistening cube into a tabletop and shut the lid. He pressed two buttons and the machine hummed. When he got closer and looked past the two standing researchers, he could see that there was a fog inside a clear plastic dome, through which he could see the flesh spinning so fast it was a blur.

Then it stopped and there was an audible *click*. An alphanumeric code appeared on the LCD screen, complete gibberish to him but, judging by the gasp of first Marnoch and then the other two, meant something significant indeed to them.

"How can that be right?" the blonde-bearded scientist said in a voice that showed confusion more than curiosity as he referenced something in a spiral-bound book. "That doesn't make sense."

"What's it say?" Chris blurted, feeling both confusion and curiosity.

"The shark …" Marnoch said, and looked again at the code, which hadn't changed, "... its tissue is suffused with a very high concentration of methamphetamine. *Very* high. And, like, *meth* meth."

"The Great White was … *tweaking?*"

"No offense, but who are you, mate?" asked the black-bearded one, who was older than Marnoch and had the hard-tanned look of a man who knew what it was to work on a boat open to the sun. "You're the one whose boat just got its seacocks opened, right?"

Asshole. "That's me." He put out his hand. "Chris Newman, captain of the *Killer Whale*."

The Ozzie shook it and said, "Not anymore, eh?" He chuckled–he *chuckled*–and added, "Rick Greene, AIMS Queensland. You've heard of it."

Lord, this guy was an ass. He was just begging for Chris to look quizzical or ask him what AIMS stood for, but Chris in his heyday had a friend who also did research for the Australian Institute of Marine Science. So he just left Rick Greene hanging. It felt good.

The yellow-bearded researcher, this one obviously fresh out of school and with a wide smile, was the one who offered his hand first this time. They shook and the kid honked in a slight Boston accent, "Pete Heyser, Woods Hole. I know who you are! You're Chris Newman, the fishing guy from that show–*The Fishing Guy!*"

"Guilty," Chris said, a little embarrassed by the gushing, "but I just want to get my last passenger safely to the island. We can swap fish tales once we're not getting jumped on by Great Wh–"

"*Marnoch! Abbie!*" Andrzej cried from above, nearly inarticulate with distress. "*Marnoch, Jesus Christ! Marnoch!*"

Marnoch was out of his seat, past the three of them, and up the ladder before Chris could even turn to take a step toward the hatch. He just traded looks with the two men down there with him, all of their expressions saying the same thing before they shook it off and made for the ladder themselves:

Oh, shit.

***

"*Status, Dre!*" Marnoch barked as soon as he got his head above the deck, and he knew something big really was happening, because Andrzej was right there to help him up faster.

"The Meg–it's tacking straight for us!" With Marnoch now up on his feet, Andrzej raced back to the helm and pointed at the radar. Marnoch ran up to it and tried to take in what it was saying, because what it was saying was that about two miles to port it was coming right at them at … *three hundred knots*.

Although Marnoch knew exactly how fast Megs swam at top speed, something the length of two school buses and the width of a tractor trailer cutting through the water faster than a bullet train made his blood turn to ice.

Before Marnoch could even shout an order, half of the Meg rose out of the water and practically flew forward, the bow wave in front of it creating a virtual tsunami of white foam. Its gray skin *whooshed* by the boat at unimaginable speed and crashed back into the water a good 120 feet past the *Participant's* stern.

It missed. The Megalodon had *missed*.

Marnoch didn't need the radar to see that the Meg was cutting a wide arc past where it had landed in the water. If the boat had been where the giant shark had landed, there wouldn't be anything left at all.

"*Hard to starboard! Now!*"

Marnoch turned to see Chris Newman practically leaping at the bridge, shouting at the top of his lungs, "For Christ's sake, man, lean into it with all you've got!"

Andrzej at the wheel seemed like he was barely holding it together and didn't need any new stress at the moment, so the famous fisherman shouldered him out of the way, hit the throttle, and threw the wheel to the right.

The *Participant* was primarily a research vessel, but the same generous funding that paid for the gear Chris had gotten giddy about meant that the boat had some serious horsepower, and the speed and strength of the epic shove to starboard had everyone on board grabbing something to maintain their balance.

"*Newman!* What are you *doing*, man?!?" Marnoch yelled, but he had already figured it out.

Marnoch didn't care if Chris Newman had fallen from grace and lost his show, lost his wife, and lost a hell of a lot of money because of those two things–the guy was a genius sailor.

The humongous dead shark draped over the starboard bow weighed almost a ton and a half and still had the deck at a thirty-degree angle and would have to be gotten off the beam if they were to sail anywhere without going in circles.

And that was what Chris was taking advantage of. He was going to run them in circles.

Marnoch was the world's leading expert in all things Megalodon; he knew even more about their behavior in the wild than did the genetic scientists who had created these new dinosaurs. And so he knew two things as surely as he knew his own name.

The first thing was that, as fast as it could cut through the water in a linear fashion, the turning radius of an aquatic animal eighty feet in length was large, indeed. The Meg hunted in straight lines, its speed and size making anything directly in its path into helpless prey. If Chris Newman ran the boat hard to starboard—with the weight of the dead shark shrinking their own smaller turning radius even more—they could elude the Meg until it tired or lost interest. They could make only incremental progress towards the island, but at least it was progress.

The other thing was that a shark that large had to get tired quickly at full speed, and trying to turn towards prey that kept turning in a smaller circle than it could match required even more energy. Chris was executing an epic rope-a-dope.

"It's working!" Marnoch yelled, and it seemed that Chris knew exactly what Marnoch meant.

With a tight smile, Chris leaned into the wheel and kept them in the tight circle. Marnoch hoped there was enough fuel left, since the *Sinker* was pulled back up almost as soon as it had been lowered into the water because of the proximity of the mass feeding frenzy around the fishing boat.

At least, Marnoch hoped that was going to be true of this one. The thing had thrown half its body *into the frickin' air*. Sure, he had personally witnessed a massive Great White do it–in fact, there was one that did it at that moment right in front of him–but Megs made even the biggest Great White look like a county fair goldfish in a plastic bag.

Something that large moving that fast and having the jolt of energy it must have taken to fling its massive body out of the water couldn't possibly keep up that level of exertion. Chris's move was perfect–since they were listing to one side anyway, turning the boat hard to starboard meant that the Meg couldn't get that beeline towards them, and it seemed that the very frenzy itself was making the creature less accurate and more wasteful of energy than it would have been if were a normal Megalodon.

Whatever "normal" meant for a Megalodon. This one's mate (where was it, anyway?) and the pups that scientists, including Marnoch, believed had been laid during the two years since the Megs escaped and so had to be cruising around somewhere, there were as many as ten of the enormous prehistoric predators. Plenty to scare the living bejesus out of shipping, but not enough to make very many confident scientific claims about.

Great Whites, the closest thing to a Megalodon that existed now, lived for sixty years, and weren't considered fully matured until they were about 25 or so. No one knew how long the cloned Megs lived, but it was almost certainly older than 60, meaning that their pups were probably still very small. So the baby Megs were probably no more than ten or fifteen feet in length right then.

Yup, just a toddler with the length and strength of a full-grown Great White. That wasn't a scary prospect, even for a paleoichthyologist.

Nope, not terrifying at all.

But they could keep this up for only so long–the *Participant* did have a steel hull, but that didn't mean it could take the strain of a ton of Great White hanging right on its side indefinitely, and there was no way it could travel in a straight line in that situation.

He stepped up to the bridge and looked intently at the radar. Yes, he could see the whitecaps where the maniac fish was thrashing about as it circled the boat, but looking at the sonar readout told him that the creature's circles were getting wider, not tighter.

It was getting tired.

"Chris, execute two more cycles and then cut the engines."

The fisherman couldn't have looked more shocked if Marnoch had told him to cover himself with chum and jump overboard. "What? What the hell are you talking about?"

We need it to get that shark off our beam. We can't get to the island with it weighing us down on one side."

"But we only need to get to the island because of this damned dinosaur." Chris didn't look particularly interested in cutting the engines, ever. "It's not going to come up and slurp the shark off this tub like a giant piece of linguine."

That actually was exactly what Marnoch thought the Meg would do. Well, not *slurp* it, but ... "Look, Chris, if you want to be at the wheel of my boat, you have to trust me. I know Megs. Even with whatever's in its system—it could be meth like the sharks and everything–it can only last so long. And we need to get that goddamn thing off the side of the boat, or we're helpless."

Chris seemed to really think it over, and Marnoch could see the exact moment when he gave in to his way of thinking. "All right," he said, "but how do we get the Meg to eat the Great White and not chomp us down with it?"

Marnoch actually smiled as he said, "That's where the great fisherman everybody knows and loves comes in."

***

"I'd say I wouldn't ask you to do anything I wouldn't do," Marnoch told Chris as Chris put on the diving gear, "but I don't want to do this. I mean, *of course* I don't want to, but I *can't* do it, because I'm in charge of the entire research mission and this boat. The crew sure as hell isn't going to do it. And I doubt you want the one survivor of your excursion to risk himself."

These were sound arguments, Chris thought, but he also thought right then that this Abbie Marnoch was a complete bastard who he'd like to frickin' strangle and throw overboard as a treat for the goddamn Meg. "To be honest, I'd really prefer if nobody had to risk themselves."

"Me too." Marnoch paused before continuing. "Anyway, when you're down in the water, timing is going to be crucial. I'm going to cut the engines just when it's at the nearest point of circling us. That way we'll drift into the curve of its trajectory in a way that it won't have any momentum, so it'll basically have to start from zero to chomp on us. I mean, on the shark."

That wasn't reassuring, Chris thought, but any reassurance at this point would just be bullshit, anyway. "So how is a speargun going to do anything that big bastard would even notice, forget about stopping it in its tracks?"

"We aren't trying to stop it in its tracks. We're just trying to get it to decide one big morsel is enough without trying to eat us as well."

"Actually, *can* it eat us? This ship has a steel hull."

"Yeah, and the Meg has meth or maybe something even worse running through its system. It might not eat us, but it could ram us … and that would pretty much be that."

"All right, all right." This conversation was actually making him wish he was already underwater. "I've spearfished before."

"Yeah, you think I haven't seen all the episodes?"

Chris laughed. "No, I thought you had a life, not spending time watching some guy who was coked out half the time yelling at fish."

At that, the smile slid off Marnoch's face. "You were … what? You always seemed so laid back."

"Well, it didn't happen before the last season, really. Or maybe it wouldn't have been the *last* season. But I had to go and …" He trailed off. How much did he want to ruin this kid's nice memories of the person he seemed to be on screen? Actually, he really was that person in the beginning, but then he started having a little bump every now and then, then more and more until … well, until what happened happened. "I'll tell you more if we don't end up as fish food, all right?"

"Deal," Marnoch said. He held up the speargun, which was truly huge. "This was made with our friend in mind. It won't kill a Meg, but it's designed to hurt it enough to, shall we say, *discourage* it from swallowing my submersible. They'd shoot it from the boat into the Meg's mouth, if they could. We've never had to try it before now."

"Why don't we shoot it from the boat this time?" Chris said, highly cognizant of the fact that he was wearing a wetsuit that would put him in the water and looking like a pretty darned munchable seal to the Megalodon.

Marnoch nodded at the question. "Thing is, it's going to be moving as slowly as we can get it to move with all the relatively tight turns and everything. If you're standing next to the Great White and it can see you, it'll aim at the boat itself and not our big dead fish friend here. If you're in the water, you can hit it right when he opens his mouth for the shark. The sudden pain will stop his forward motion and make him kind of drift into and land his teeth onto the shark, enough to grab it and pull it off the side of the *Participant*. At least, that's the theory."

Chris sighed and said, "A theory's better than nothing, I guess."

"That's the *Fishing Guy* spirit!" Marnoch said with real joy, and Chris kind of wanted to punch him in the face for it. "Go down the ladder into the water here, and scoot far enough away from our late friend so the Meg doesn't take you with it when it grabs ol' Brucie."

"Then what?"

"Right, sorry–as soon as it opens its mouth, fire into its cheek. Right into the mouth, past the teeth, into the inside cheek. That'll make it start closing its mouth but not before it can grab the Great White and yank it off the side of the boat."

That sounded like a lot of hope and not a lot of solid sense. But it was all they had, wasn't it? If they didn't do it, the monster was *definitely* going to take them down, either by being able to curb its turning radius and just eating them in its weird frenzy or by waiting for them to run out of gas and drift helplessly until the Meg could get a nice head of speed up and demolish the boat and eat its spilled contents like it was some kind of seafaring piñata.

"Ready?"

"Let's say I am."

Marnoch smiled, but it was obvious that he knew this was the least garbage solution they could think of to a very garbage situation. And, as he descended the ladder that, thankfully, the shark's giant carcass hadn't flopped onto, Chris accepted that he was the only celebrated fisherman in a five-hundred-mile radius and he had gone spearfishing many times, only sometimes for the show. So yeah, he guessed he was the man for the job.

But Jesus, what a job.

He fell backwards into the water pulled down by the scuba gear, still cold as hell despite the wet suit, and settled into place a couple of yards away from the shark's corpse, which didn't quite reach the surface hanging off the boat. He fitted his mask and put the second stage of the scuba regulator in his mouth, found his bearings, and positioned himself with the speargun.

He could feel when Marnoch had Andrzej cut the engine, the slight centrifugal force pressing on him from the hull immediately ceasing.

They were dead in the water. Hopefully not literally.

There with his ears underwater with the rest of him, he could actually hear the Meg gurgling and churning in the ocean just a hundred or so feet away. The water was hard to see through even at this shallow depth, but then ... there it was.

He had never seen the leviathan in the flesh before, and Christ, he wished he wasn't seeing it now. The size of it was just unbelievable, truly–it looked closer than it could really have been, which was good, because if it *was* as close as it looked, he'd already be dead.

Why was he down there, anyway? This was Marnoch's research mission, Marnoch was the Megalodon expert, why wasn't *he* down there?

Chris knew the simple answer: Marnoch wasn't expendable, and the second-most–qualified person on board was Chris himself. He actually *did* have spearfishing experience, but that was with fish like yellowtail or grouper, not predators, and certainly not frickin' enormous things like sharks or, God knew, a Megalodon.

However, the object here wasn't to kill it with the spear–that was well-nigh impossible and stupid to try anyway if it weren't–but just to distract it enough somewhere sensitive to get it to leave off trying to destroy their boat. Belay "trying"–it would definitely succeed.

But deflecting the thing or even slowing it down was all Chris could hope for, according to Marnoch, and that was fine by him. He didn't have any experience with removing a Great White from the beam of a boat, but who the hell *did?*

He didn't have radio or any other kind of contact with Marnoch or anyone else topside, so as the Meg came right towards him, it was up to him and him alone to shoot the spear into this damned thing's mouth and hope for the best. One way, he'd be alive, and the other, he'd probably be crushed to death before he even knew what was happening.

***

Andrzej remained at the helm while Marnoch stayed on deck and watched the Megalodon approach. Under any other circumstances–other, perhaps, than being in the submersible in the creature's line of travel–this would have been an amazing, proud moment for the paleoichthyologist, a chance to study the creature up close with every scientific instrument aboard. But now it was one of pure anxiety, if not terror.

He looked at the twenty-something survivor from Chris Newman's fishing expedition, his name was Jamie Cant, Marnoch had learned. (*A very Gen-Z name if ever I heard one* popped into Marnoch's head, and he had to shake it off.) Jamie seemed mesmerized with horror but also with a young man's morbid excitement as the gigantic shape under the water moved closer and closer off to starboard. He had earlier been transfixed on the Great White folded over the side, but now he was looking at something even bigger and even deadlier.

The crew, some of the most experienced and adept around, joined the college kid in staring at the Meg approaching. There was nothing else for them to do–Chris was positioned next to the dead shark's tail in the hope that the leviathan would be interested in the corpse even though it was largely out of the water. Andrzej had gotten them into position and now stood uselessly at the controls. And Marnoch himself could do nothing but wait and hope that the once-famous fisherman still had it in him to shoot straight.

***

Chris breathed as evenly as he could through the regulator, which was best for using the scuba gear and also for staying as calm as possible instead of getting more and more freaked out. Also, he had hunted tiger and bull sharks for his program before. (Never with a speargun, but still.).

There were a few scenarios here, only one of which was positive. First and best was that he was able to shoot the monster right at the gums or in the cheek, the most sensitive parts according to Abbie Marnoch, who was the person who knew best in the world. That would dissuade the thing from continuing forward, sparing the boat from capsizing and throwing everyone into the angry-predator–filled waters.

Second, and nowhere near as good, would be that the Meg got shot and attacked the boat with less enthusiasm than it would have. It was already acting more aggressively than Marnoch said he had ever seen, so at least slowing its momentum towards the boat could mean they'd probably be able to stay afloat long enough to somehow get back to the safety of solid ground on Persuasion Island. Marnoch hadn't said, but Chris was happy to assume that the Meg would be in enough distracting pain to keep it from making a second attack. But the thing was crazy, it seemed–was there meth in it as well? How much goddamn meth would it take to make a Megalodon as frantic as all the other fish they had encountered were?

A good question for Marnoch … if they survived.

The last, and worst, scenario that could happen would be that he either missed the Meg's mouth entirely or shot it somewhere in its two-inch–thick hide that didn't really bother it, if at all. In that case, Chris would definitely be chomped on or sucked in– he couldn't decide which would be worse–and the boat would almost certainly be destroyed, making a lovely smorgasbord of every soul aboard.

Which would it be? There was one way to find out.

It was hard to estimate underwater how close the Meg was, since its enormous size wasn't something Chris (or anyone) was really used to. But its terrifying visage was becoming less blue and more distinct by the second, and it was now or never.

It must have been very near the boat, indeed, since its mouth started opening to chomp just as

Chris pulled the trigger and a blast of compressed gas shot the spear at terrific speed directly at the pitch-black maw.

All Chris heard was an explosion of bubbles as the Meg shook its entire body at the pain of the huge spear stabbing right into its upper gums. *Yes!* Chris cheered in his head, and he could hear the screams of celebration right through the boat's hull and across the few feet of water.

It took only a second for him to realize that the screams of joy were actually shouts of dismay and horror.

The Meg was too big to stop on a dime. Too big to stop in time to avoid the boat. But it did slow down quite a bit and its mouth was now clamped shut as it headed straight for the side of the *Participant*'s hull. However, when it was hit it had immediately started into a dive, and so the boat didn't get the full brunt of the impact.

Its snout hit the boat under the waterline and shoved it forward with great force. If it had been off center by even a little bit more, it would have been sent into a spin with the hull smashing right into Chris instead of pushing the entire vessel away from him.

The force of the blow, along with the thirty-degree angle of the deck pointed toward the Meg, was enough to fling the dead Great White off the side of the boat and flopping into the sea like a surfboard *splatting* against still water.

Chris was looking back at the boat now and could see the Meg continuing its dive into the deep, leaving the boat to ricochet away from where the boat had suddenly been liberated of two tons of shark hard to port, then back to starboard with less momentum, then back to port before finally settling into a gentle rocking that finally stopped.

It was horrible enough to watch from under the water, the hull of the boat sliding sideways, then rocking back and forth like a toy in a bathtub. But judging by the shouts of the men aboard the boat, it must have felt like the most pants-filling carnival ride in history.

The shark started sinking to the bottom, blood streaming after it like dark maroon taffy being stretched behind it.

When Chris saw what happened next, he turned his back on it and scrambled like a maniac to the ladder in the water. If he didn't move right then– like, *right* then–he would no doubt suffer the same fate as the sinking carcass of that Great White. But it was almost impossible not to watch the gory spectacle.

What seemed like every predator that had finished off the *Killer Whale* suddenly returned, zooming from the black depths to meet the dead shark at full speed, ripping and tearing chunks off of it, whole pieces of belly and head and tail, momentarily stopping its descent and even lifting it up as they pulled off the chunks and swallowed them and went back for more. And there–

JESUS CHRIST! Furious bubbles exploded from the regulator.

A six-foot tiger shark appeared out of nowhere and came right at Chris. He practically jumped onto the rails of the metal ladder and hurled himself upwards.

As four hands reached down and grabbed him and hauled him into the boat, he still couldn't help looking back at the carnage. All that was visible from the surface, however, was the white caps of the agitated water above the frenzied feast happening below.

Then he remembered–*the Megalodon!*

He whipped around to see the Meg making a wide turn that could only be heading back to them– or, rather, to the bloodbath in the water. But he wasn't the only one.

Pretty much exactly when Chris noticed what Meg was doing, he heard Marnoch practically scream, *"FULL SPEED HEADING TO PERSUASION ISLAND!"*

Andrzej was on it, and by the time the Megalodon got back and started taking part in the feast of not only what was left of the shark but also of the predator that themselves were chewing and churning there, the *Participant* was already well underway.

***

Marnoch didn't bother to say more into the VHF radio and put the handset down. "Coast Guard isn't sending any boats out where there's an active Meg in the area," he said to Andrzej. "I guess I can't really blame them."

"That's bull," Andrzej scoffed. "This is a vessel in distress." The captain was keeping the boat on course to the island, which was only about an hour away now. Things were calm, and the dinosaur shark hadn't made another appearance, which made sense for a Meg, but there was no telling what apex predators would do when they were hopped up on methamphetamines.

Marnoch had tried and tried to figure out how these deepwater fish would ever encounter enough of the street drug to have it in their very tissue he cut out of one at random. That Great White had freaking *thrown itself* out of the water at the boat. He had seen sharks jump after bait and even leave the water entirely when in a serious frenzy, but never had he seen a Great White do it nor had he ever seen one jump so high and so far. And he didn't know Megs could even lift so much as their snouts out of the water.

He supposed amphetamines would do that to a creature, but hell. And the Megalogon–had that ingested some of it as well? Is that why Chris had to shoot it in the first place to keep it from ramming them full bore and straight on? Marnoch wasn't surprised that the fisherman had nailed the shot–he really had watched every episode of Chris's show– but it really had been a thing of beauty.

It took him a moment to identify what it was he was hearing. It started off barely audible over the waves, but then became unmistakably the rhythmic chopping of helicopter blades.

"The Coast Guard sent *cMarnochs!*" Andrzej cried with relief. "I thought you said they weren't coming at all?"

Marnoch squinted at the horizon to the south. He could see the tiny shape of the still-distant cMarnoch, but already it looked too large and too dark to be a USCG aircraft. "I did, and I don't think they are, Dre."

"What? Then who is that? I mean, I don't really care who comes to help, but who the hell is it if it's not them?"

"Don't know. But we're about to find out. Get everybody below, just in case."

"In case what?"

"Exactly," Marnoch said, his eyes not leaving the shape growing on the horizon.

***

"Who is that?" El Gato barked through the comm on his helmet at the co-pilot in the front seat. He was where the gunner would sit in the Mi-8MT former armed gunship when it still had active weapons, but, unlike his submarines, the helicopter had been decommissioned. It was still cool as hell, though, Gato always thought. "Is that one of Jalisco's boats? God, I wish we could shoot a missile at them." Jalisco was his biggest rival.

"No, *jefe*, it's a research-type vessel. See the little submersible on deck?"

Gato did see it, and relaxed a bit. It still would have been fun to blow them up, although there was already something seriously wrong with one side of the ship. It looked bent, crunched, like some giant hand had landed a hard karate chop right on the starboard side.

"Weird. There doesn't seem to be anybody aboard but the one at the controls, *jefe*."

"Maybe the Megalodon ate all of them," Gato said with a hearty laugh that, after a moment's consideration, the two pilots echoed. "Anyway, who cares–how long until the island?"

"Fifteen minutes, *jefe*."

"Bring us down on the far side, away from the marina."

"You mean at the helipad?" The last part belied the pilot's realization that he had said basically *You mean like always?*

Gato let it go. It was a little unnecessary to say, but he couldn't really have the pilot shot because first, he was his goddamn pilot, and second, because that probably would be hard on the morale of the other men on board. "Bring us in, *muchacho*, and let's get to it. We have a submarine to find, eh?"

***

The two men inside the *Buceadora* deep in the stomach of the Megalodon–Manny had indeed freaked out once he regained consciousness, with imaginary spiders crawling all over and inside him, but Davi had already handcuffed his wrists and ankles around a pipe. It wasn't very far from him, but it was far enough while Manny rode it out.

He was counting down the hours–really the minutes, as there wasn't anything else to do except wait to be digested and die in a truly gruesome fashion that he didn't want to spend his remaining time on Earth thinking about.

The lights on the sub were still working fine; it would be a while before the lack of power production via electrolysis from the seawater drained the batteries. There was Manny, shaking and sometimes shrieking to aft. And there was the drugs, plenty left after the meth had been dumped. Davi would have thought the meth would have been plenty to affect the whale, but apparently they would have to get into the cocaine after all, consequences from El Gato be damned. One in the hand worth more than two in the bush and all that.

He was about to call it when there was a huge rush of seawater by the sound of it and large objects–relatively soft rather than metal or the plexiglass of a sea vessel–started slapping against the hull of the *Buceadora*.

The thing was eating something, or, rather, had just eaten it. By the sound of it, two loud wet slaps, it was something in two sizable chunks. Davi instantly guessed that it was a shark, a really big one, maybe even a Great White, that had been torn in half. It was eating, obviously, and not too long after a rash of new, smaller slaps came against the hull. These could have been anything, but the Megalodon had had a real effect on the shark population in that part of the Pacific, so it was probably sharks and other creatures not used to being anywhere but at the top of the food chain. They didn't know to, and maybe not even how to or why to, get away from something that was planning on eating *them*. It was kind of like watching some *motociclista muy macho* get his ass handed to him by a *luchador* in a foul mood at some sleazy *barra*.

So the Meg was still eating. That meant it wasn't, in fact, going to vomit them up. The incredible volume of meth they had loaded into the decompression chamber and shot out into the water inside the monster's stomach, somehow, unbelievably, hadn't been enough.

Davi stared at the cocaine packed neatly in the hold. The rows of soft bags were almost too pretty, not just in terms of how they looked but also how much they were worth and how extremely they could affect the human body. A single kilo of the stuff was *way* more than enough to drop even the biggest human.

But of course that wasn't what they were dealing with here. The Meg hadn't gotten agitated enough by the meth, but Davi certainly didn't want to kill the thing with himself still inside. And he also didn't want to use too much of the coke because El Gato would definitely be taking every gram lost out of his hide. Maybe there was a sweet spot to get the thing to empty its stomach–he suddenly wished he knew something, anything, about shark anatomy. Could the things even vomit them up? He had to believe they could or he would open one of the packages and snort and swallow enough of it to kill a *fútbol* team, get himself good and dead before the thing digested the sub and him along with it.

No, he had to assume the thing could get sick. It seemed to wash out some water and also some of the things in its stomach. But how to dose the big *bastardo* so it got enough but not too much, and that he used as little of the cocaine as possible so Gato didn't put his head on a goddamn pike once he escaped the Meg, that was the challenge.

He got a pencil and the back of a map and started making calculations; he had *no* idea whether they were accurate or not. But it did make the time pass while he waited and vacillated on what to do and how to do it.

He did know it would be a lot more than one two-kilo package, so he placed the first one into the decompression chamber and jettisoned it into the blackness of the thing's stomach. Got the party started, then went back to his useless figures.

**

El Gato beat both submarines to the island by a long shot. The Mi-8MT carrying him, the pilots, and ten machine-gun–toting soldiers landed on the far side of the island, which was less than a mile from the other beach. It was small, but there was plenty of activity on both ends.

The research craft that they had flown over in the helicopter was something he had never seen on his occasional flights to and from the island, and the pilot reported that he hadn't noticed it before either, and they kept a close track on what vessels used the islands. It was almost entirely fishing crafts and boats taking partiers and the odd surfing party in or out, as there really wasn't much on the island to offer "civilians" other than a good home base for enjoying the good life. The rock wasn't owned by any private entity, and it wasn't useful enough to the United States to be claimed, so it was nominally under the Mexican flag.

Gato supposed that if it had been the Americans, no one would have been able to make it a smuggler's way station, and the US drinking age of 21 couldn't have been so flagrantly flouted. It was kind of a win-win for everybody, as long as the two sides didn't ever really meet.

The Mi-8MT made a perfect landing, and Gato clapped the pilot on the shoulder, which made the man start in his seat and then take a breath of relief. Everybody was so jumpy around him! It was just as he liked it.

The men exited the cMarnoch and took positions of protection around the vehicle with two following El Gato to the tunnel. There was planning to do on how they were supposed to get the cocaine out of a sixty-foot sea monster, and the office carved out of the rock would be the command center. Gato always liked a little razzle-dazzle, and nobody else had a goddamned *office* at their smuggled tunnels, not even Jalisco.

Being dragged by one of the men was someone he had almost forgotten about: the *gringo*, Spence, the Scripps Institution guy his team had abducted from Universidad Nacional Autónoma de Mexico. He was a world-renowned expert on sharks and whatnot, and he would probably be able to tell them all about the Megalodon, or at least enough to help them get the metal meal out of him. Then they could let him go or kill him or whatever–he had been blindfolded and stayed that way after they grabbed him, put him on the helicopter, and flew him there, so they didn't really *have* to kill him. But the boys were working hard and they could use a bit of fun. He hadn't decided yet and right now didn't care about some stupid fish scientist once the guy stopped being useful.

Gato sat in his very comfortable leather chair, incongruous like the rest of the office in a dark tropical tunnel, and the man was plopped down and his blindfold removed. He looked, not unreasonably in Gato's eyes, a bit disoriented and maybe scared out of his considerable wits.

"*Hola*, Señor Scientist," Gato said with not a little smugness, "you might be wondering what you are doing here, eh?"

It was hard to tell if the man was nodding by the way he was looking around the room, seeming more interested in his surroundings than in responding. Gato decided to go with the nod.

"Well, wonder no more, *mi amigo*. You are here to tell us about this Megalodon. You know, the monster shark? You are a shark scientist? You are

Doctor George Spence, *sí?*" He waited roughly a nanosecond before barking, "Let's go! Speak!"

"Yes!" he shouted at an involuntary volume he seemed slightly abashed about. "I am very curious about, um, what exactly I'm doing here. Where am I, anyway?" The very tan man's curiosity about his situation actually seemed to calm him. He really *was* a scientist, wasn't he?

"Don't worry about where you are, Doctor Spence. Worry about *why* you are here."

"Yes, that's what I said earlier: I am very curious, indeed. Why am I here? Why did you kidnap me and put me on a helicopter and then take me onto an island and now inside some kind of tunnel on the island?"

"What the–? How do you know that?"

Spence, weirdly, didn't seem to think it was a big deal. "And you are … ?"

"Mister Gato," Gato said. "I mean, I am *El* Gato."

"The drug kingpin? That is very interesting." He cleared his throat. "In any case, Mister El Gato, I spend a lot of time on seafaring vessels doing research, especially in this part of the Pacific a few hundred miles off the California coast. I don't have the slightest idea what island I'm on, but I imagine it's one of those uninhabited pieces of land frequented–obviously–by smugglers and also used by party boats doing deep-sea fishing excursions."

"Holy shit!" Gato said. "Should I just kill you now?"

Spence said calmly, "No, that isn't necessary. I don't care a whit for the War on Drugs, I say live and let live and all that. Now, you brought me here for a reason, ostensibly something to do with sharks. I don't know why the abduction was strictly necessary–I mean, *try* to get a scientist not to talk about his work, right?"

Gato stared at him, almost unable to comprehend what he was looking at. "You are not scared?"

"On the contrary, I am utterly terrified and in fear for my life," Spence said in a tone that said anything but. "However, I figure the best way to save myself is by providing whatever service it is that you need from a biologist who studies sharks. So … what may I do for you in order to convince you to spare my life?"

"We, um … um, we have a Megalodon."

"I see. They are–at least the ones that were cloned from ancient DNA–much like sharks, although of course much larger. Ironically, perhaps, the specimens that we currently have seem much more docile than Great Whites or even tiger or bull sharks. Of course, Doctor Marnoch would be the man to talk about when it comes to Megalodons. I believe he was conducting an expedition very near here to study the big guys. Have you been in contact with his Institute?"

"We have not, *amigo*," Gato said, remembering the strange boat they flew over, the one with the little submersible on top. "But he would be the man to talk to?"

"Oh, yes," Spence said. "I have a great deal I can help you with regarding sharks in general, but when it comes to Megalodons in particular, Marnoch's your man."

"*Gracias*," El Gato said, motioned for the soldier to hand him his pistol. and shot Spence through the heart. Before the body had even slumped to the floor, he said to one of the armed soldiers, "Did you notice that boat we flew over on the way here? The one that looked damaged on the one side?"

"*Sí*, El Gato."

"It looked like it was headed for this island, would you say?"

"*Sí*, El Gato."

"*Bueno*. They must be in distress, whatever that damage on the side was. And there must be people aboard, or it wouldn't be moving under power toward the island, you see?"

"*Sí*, El Gato."

"Yes … and I bet one of those people is this Doctor Marnoch, the Megalodon man, right?"

"*Sí*, El Gato."

"All right, get your men together. As soon as Pedro gets here in the *Flotadora*, we're going over to the other side of the island to have a talk with this Marnoch. Got it?"

"*Sí*, El Gato."

"Carry on, then."

"*Sí*, El Gato."

He always enjoyed taking the time to talk with his soldiers. It made him a better boss.

He smiled at the bloodied body of the shark scientist–*stupido* no matter what degree he may have had–and called for someone to come clean up the mess.

***

Enough time had passed since the Megalodon attack that Marnoch, Greene, Heyser, and Chris allowed themselves to go topside to join Andrzej, who looked none the worse for wear. Herser and Greene went to occupy themselves with shipboard tasks. The kid, Cant, just shook his head distantly when asked if he wanted to join them.

Which was fine, Chris decided. The hold wasn't inherently safer than on deck, but it was probably better for everyone if the poor guy wasn't further traumatized by seeing a swordfish or a grouper or, hell, a goddamn *dolphin* at this point.

"How long have we got, Cap?" Chris said to Andrzej at the helm, who from what Chris could see had done an admirable job keeping the boat on course with a gigantic dent in its side. It definitely changed the aquadynamics of the vessel, but according to Chris's glance at the instruments, somehow the sailor kept it true.

"Half an hour?" he said, a noticeable amount of question in his voice. "It's hard to keep a steady heading and a regular speed, you know? But we should be able to see land in a little bit here. I don't think we're at the point where we could miss it."

Almost unconsciously, each man made sure to find a spot of wood in the cabin and touch it.

"Nothing to do now but wait," he added. "We can assess damage when we get to the marina."

Chris let out a laugh. "More of a dock than a marina. There might be ten boats and some other personal watercraft, nothing to write home about. There are some kids who know how to operate a boat, and they bring the others out. There's also a couple of boats that ferry them over. The sailors with those boats usually just stay in their huts and drink all weekend."

"Jesus. Ah well, at this point, we'll take what we can get." This made the three of them let out a rueful chuckle.

"So, Chris," Marnoch started hesitantly, "do you mind me asking what your story is? It seems like *The Fishing Guy* just suddenly went dark. You had the whole shark hunting episode during Shark Week, and then you were gone."

"Nah, ask away. There hasn't been a *Behind the Music* or anything on *The Fishing Guy* or me." Chris looked out to sea before continuing. "The fact is, this whole meth stuff we're encountering brings it all back anyway. The fame, the money, the women that *The Fishing Guy* brought me–it all became too much for a guy who really was all about the angling, you know?"

Marnoch could not have looked more shocked if someone had told him Santa Claus was real and had been hiding during the off-months all these years as a shape-shifting porpoise with a handlebar mustache and a monocle. "*You?*"

"I know, right? Even though the show was all over basic cable and YouTube, I still was just a fisherman at heart. Deep-sea was what I loved and it still is what turns these rich kids on the most."

Saying those words sent a nauseating shock through Chris's system as he remembered five of the "rich kids" he was charged with keeping safe were now dead. And not just dead, but ripped apart and consumed by tweaking sharks.

"You okay?" Andrzej asked.

Chris nodded, choking back tears. "Yeah, so the thing is, you go out deep-sea fishing, you're out for the day. It's not like lake fishing where you can say screw it and call it a day after a few hours of catching nothing, and catching nothing is mostly the name of the game on the open ocean. But when you get one and fight it and bring it in–could be eating size, could be trophy size, you don't know until it leaps out of the water and fights you–all that time waiting just disappears and you're in the moment. You guys fish?"

They both shook their heads, but Marnoch seemed shocked at the very idea that a marine biologist, paleoichthy or otherwise, would injure or kill one of the ocean's magnificent creatures.

"No, sure, I get that," Chris answered himself. "But yeah, there's a lot of time where you're just sitting there, you and the boat captain and a mate, maybe, the camera crew and maybe the guest fisherman. I didn't know anything about drugs other than a little weed now and then. Hell, I didn't even do that until it became legal in California."

"So some non-union camera and sound guys and some washed-up celebrities?" Marnoch said.

Chris laughed. "How'd you know they weren't union?"

"I've been around documentary crews, and I figured the channel saved money on it because you filmed in international waters. But kind of a lower-echelon production crew and has-been actors or whatever? I mean, no offense, but that sounds like a recipe for trouble."

"Naw, I get you. We used union for the land-based stuff, of course, but yeah, it was younger guys or sometimes older guys who had been drummed out of the union for whatever reason. And add in a David Lee Roth or Ray Liotta, and you got a perfect storm, man. But I'll tell you what, Tawny Kitaen, God bless her soul, knew how to catch a giant sea bass and reel it in *on her own*."

Both Marnoch and Andrzej were appropriately impressed. That had been a hell of a show, maybe one of the best in the whole run. Tawny had reeled in that giant bass by herself and then, of course, Chris and the boat crew helped her pull it in and cut the line and everything. Chris thought he remembered catching something pretty nice, but he wasn't entirely sure if that even made it into the final cut after Tawny's amazing battle.

"But yeah, bored TV guys who didn't have to worry about violating union rules, plus former big deals–I'm not saying Tawny or Ray or anyone else in particular, but as a group–they had drugs. Lord, did they have drugs."

Andrzej shook his head. Even at forty, the man was an old salt and never would have trucked with drug use on his boat, whether the tub actually belonged to him or not.

"So I started with a little bump now and then during the extra slow times waiting for something to bite. These were times when nothing spectacular or likely to follow the boat were showing up on sonar. I didn't drink during a shoot and neither did the crew; that was a rule I had, because if you got sloppy out there, somebody could end up drunk and falling overboard right in the middle of a shot, which would ruin an entire week's worth of planning."

"Damn right, it could," Andrze interjected. He didn't even drink on board.

"But coke? That was a different story. That made everyone hyper-aware and on point whenever something did get caught, I guess *if* something got caught while we were messed up. I can't remember if Tawny was on marching powder when she got that bass, but I know for a fact some of the other guest stars were coked up hard when they performed some superhuman feats of deep-sea fishing."

Marnoch said, "I've never done anything like that–weed, hell yes, even shrooms, but no narcotics. What the heck happened to take you up from an occasional snort or two?"

"Well, that's the thing. One bump to join the crowd when there was nothing to really shoot, maybe we had already gotten enough B-roll and such, killing time until something happened, but then that became two, then three, then more and more, to the point where I was losing interest in whether we actually hauled in anything that day or not. I just wanted to hit the drugs almost as soon as we left port."

"Oh, no."

"*Oh no* is right. I started faking it, not worrying about actually catching anything but instead showing me or the guest 'fighting' something and then using old, unused footage to make it look like we brought something in."

"The guest fishers went along with this?"

"Who do you think came up with the idea?" Chris sort of laughed. "I mean, they or the crew were the ones who brought the drugs in the first place. I had no idea where to buy street drugs–I was just a fisherman who got lucky and got his own show. No, it was really starting to affect my work and I was heading for a breaking point. People were starting to talk, as TV people do, union or not."

Andrzej shot Chris a look, one Chris recognized as the ultimate side-eye. It was a little rude from someone he had just really met, but he knew he deserved it.

"You're right, Cap. It was incredibly wrong for anyone aboard a boat to put everyone else in danger, whether physically or with their career. But there I was on the day one of the sound guys brought some crystal meth."

"Aw, hell," Marnoch said, and not admiringly. "That's hardcore."

"Yeah, that was the beginning of the end. One hit of that stuff and I didn't care where I was, who I was, or what was even happening on the boat. It was the most horrifying, most euphoric experience I've ever had. You know you're in trouble when goddamn *Cuba Gooding, Jr.* is trying to talk you down."

Marnoch looked like he was both dying to say something and trying his hardest not to say it. Finally he asked, "What does it feel like? I hate to ask, but you know, I *am* a scientist. I have to collect data."

Chris and Marnoch both laughed, but Andrzej looked like he'd like nothing more than to hurl himself overboard and swim to shore. Chris said, "You saw those sharks and grouper and the rest, right? The Great White that flung itself onto the side of the boat and kept snapping until it died?"

Marnoch nodded with foreboding.

"It felt like that."

"Jesus."

"Yeah, exactly. But the growing negligence wasn't even what did it." Chris steeled himself and continued, "No, one day we had both coke *and* meth on board, and I got cooked on the meth before the boat even left the dock. Then we went out and it was an *agonizing* six hours and we hadn't even gotten a nibble from a barracuda. I was bored, Tom Sizemore was bored, and God knows the crew was bored."

Andrzej interrupted with an annoyed, low-key, "Land ho."

Chris turned and saw the dark shape just at the horizon. He'd been back and forth to Persuasion Island enough times to know that's what it was even without the navigational aids or Andrzej's petulant announcement.

"So what happened?" Marnoch asked, obviously anxious to get to the chewy center of the story before they docked. "You were on meth, and then …"

"And then I decided to do a couple of lines of coke to top it off."

"God, that's what I thought you were going to say."

"Yep. Some $14,000 cameras went into the drink, the boom operator and I started punching each other, and even Sizemore went below decks to get away from the craziness." Chris shook his head, seeing the scene in his mind for the thousandth time, or the ten-thousandth. It wasn't like getting drunk, where everything became a blur if you could remember anything at all–no, he could replay every single second of his freakout in excruciating detail. He wished he couldn't.

"Did you get arrested?"

"No. International waters, and besides, the others were blitzed out of their heads as well. But I only did these drugs when I was on a shoot, so I didn't have access to them and didn't have the tolerance those guys had. By the time I got home that night, the channel had pulled the show. I thought my agent was going to murder me for blowing a gig that was *literally* me getting out on a boat and going fishing.

Everything ended that day … including me and drugs. I haven't touched anything since." He let out a sigh. "Not even weed."

"Thank God," Andrzej said. "I, for one, am glad to still have you in the world."

"See? And he just met me." He looked at the boat captain with gratitude. "I'm a nice guy, people like me when I'm not on freakin' drugs. So I started the charter based out of San Diego, taking the trust fund kids out from Persuasion for fishing and fun, sometimes with organizers of the whole trip. They've all seen the show running a million times a day on the channel, so there's that. It lets me forget the celebrity and that crap and just get back to fishing. But once you've had that, once you've had the money and the women and the fame … I'm always a little sad. Always."

"That is a consequence of meth," Andrzej said. "It gets into your pleasure center and raises the level where you can feel anything. You start chasing that dragon."

Marnoch looked at his boat captain. "Dre, I've never seen you like this. What is with you and drugs? I've never seen you take so much as a Tylenol."

"Family." Andrzej drew a deep breath and let it out. "Meth and cocaine, just as Mister Newman says. I had to shoot my own brother in the chest with a flare gun when he did both and went on a rampage. He came after my daughter–five years old!–on a pleasure cruise on my own skiff. He fell dead into the water and we had to fish his body out with a net. So yes, I have a slight problem with people doing drugs. I can't imagine what would happen if one of these tweaking sharks also ingested coke along with the meth you detected, Abbie."

After a very awkward silence that seemed to last for hours as they approached the island, Marnoch said, "I'm sorry, Dre, I don't know what to say about what happened. But it's over with the fish, However meth got into the water, they seem to have calmed down. We don't have to worry about that trigger for both of you guys anymore."

"Um, Marnoch? Captain? Do you guys see this?"

After a few seconds, Chris could see that they both definitely saw it.

Two men with machine guns stood on the dock waiting for them. Four more armed men in paramilitary gear were spread where the dock met the shore.

"Smugglers," Chris said. "They use the island … but I've never seen them in person. They stick to the other end of the island, is what I've always heard. I don't let the kids go that way."

"But they're on this side now?" Marnoch said. "Why?"

Chris swallowed back his fear and said, "I have no idea. But it's too late to turn back, so I guess we're about to find out."

***

Marnoch had heard of drug smugglers using this island, of course, but he'd never had cause to stop at Persuasion; the *Participant* was well provisioned for days at sea, since it worked in depths for the submersible as they went out to find the two Megalodons and see if they could catch a glimpse of the pups as well. They had tracking devices on the Megs, of course, but the radios sent readable transmissions only when the animals were somewhat near the surface and the ship was within a mile or so of where they were. A mile radius wasn't much on the open sea, but even though the Megs were brand-new in the present-day environment, and despite the fact that their hard-wiring was for life 3 million years ago, they still seemed to follow the same routes with some regularity. The submersible was able to detect them better under the water than the surface ship could, but then of course there was the danger of being slurped up by the

Meg. Well, Marnoch always thought, there was no gain without challenge, especially when it came to ocean-based research.

This challenge was outside his wheelhouse, however. With nowhere to go but the dock, armed soldiers or not, Andrzej brought the *Participant* in perfectly and got it anchored and tied.

In a thick Mexican accent, one of the soldiers stepped right up to the boat and said, "We are looking for Mister Marnoch."

Ice suddenly flowed through Marnoch's veins, and he wanted nothing more in that moment than to dive into the sea and never look back. But what could he do? "I'm Marnoch."

"The dinosaur fish scientist?"

Close enough, he thought. "Yes. *Sí*."

"You will come with us."

"Okay, but leave them alone?" he said, indicating his shipmates.

The two soldiers on the dock looked back to the four on shore. They exchanged looks and as good as shrugged. "No, let's bring them, too. *Jefe* will decide what to do."

Chris spoke up, "There are thirty college students on this island, and I'm the one responsible for them. I have to stay behind." He gave Marnoch an apologetic look, but it wasn't necessary–he thought that was the exact right thing to do.

The main soldier asked Marnoch, "It will be noticed if he is gone?"

Marnoch nodded. "He is the one in charge of their trip. They will radio to the mainland if he doesn't show up." This was a bluff on his part–he highly doubted that any of the partiers on the island even knew there *was* VHF radio equipment on the island, much less knew how to contact anyone on it. Cellphones were useless this far from land, and, even though he didn't know anything about the undoubtedly air-conditioned huts or other structures set up for the vacationers, he assumed nobody had a satellite hookup.

"The radio," the soldier said, and moved his head to direct the other standing on the dock to board the boat. "*Destruir la radio.*"

That was enough of a cognate for Marnoch to shut his eyes in self-recrimination. He just *had* to mention the radio, didn't he? *Idiot*. Within moments, he could hear the second soldier smashing the onboard radio.

The first soldier said to Chris, "You know where the radio is with your people?"

Marnoch could see Chris calculate what he would say, then give up for the safety of his charges. "Yes. I'll get it."

"You have five minutes, *amigo*." He motioned to one of the soldiers on land. "*Sigue al gringo. Mantente fuera de la vista*," and said to Chris, "That means to follow you but stay out of sight. You get the radio, you do not send anything, you bring it back here, *claro?*"

"*Claro*," Chris said, looking pale. "Just don't hurt the kids, okay?"

"That is up to you, Mister."

The soldier stepped aside to allow Chris to get off the boat and walk down the wooden dock, where the other soldier waited for him. Then they began the trudge toward the makeshift village Marnoch imagined was just around the copse of tropical trees.

The first soldier barked some orders at the four remaining minions and took Marnoch roughly by the arm. The other soldiers came forward and in seconds had in tow Andrzej, Heyser, Greene, and the kid, Cant, who looked like he had gone to his happy place never to return.

"*Vamos*," he snapped, and they started their march across the island.

It took less than half an hour to get to the enclave, but going over the rocks, through hard-packed sand, and between randomly placed trees made it feel much longer to Marnoch. Also, walking towards what felt like certain doom added a few apparent hours to the march.

Once at their destination on the opposite shore, Marnoch was separated from the rest of the group and brought to the tunnel. He was amazed at the camouflage hiding the entrance, and then at the tunnel itself. The smugglers weren't kidding around with this stuff. He wasn't much for skullduggery himself, but he admired it greatly for its necessary innovation, and this was a premium example created by very wealthy people looking to make a great deal more.

The two soldiers who had been standing on the dock when they arrived now rather roughly brought him past the camouflage of foliage and fake rocks and into the tunnel itself. He was floored by what looked to be a large office room complete with desk chair, table, and visitor chairs. There was a computer. There was a wall like an office cubicle onto which what Marnoch had to guess were reconnaissance photos and maps were pinned.

Sitting behind the desk was a peculiar man. The swarthy gentleman wasn't dressed in any kind of uniform or paramilitary regalia, instead dressed in an open-collared white shirt and sporting a thick gold chain.

"You are Mister Marnoch?" the man asked, his Mexican accent almost as an added flavor to his speech rather than thick like those of his lackeys. "The Megalogon scientist?"

"Megalo*don*, yes. And with whom might I be speaking?"

"How polite! I cannot share my identity, but you may know me as El Gato."

Ah! But is that not your identity, even if it's not your birth name? Marnoch thought, but let that go as a bad job. He knew who El Gato was because it was impossible for sailors not to know at least the monikers of the drug smugglers off the coast of Baja California and Mexico. "I would say it's a pleasure to meet you, but I'm afraid I need to know what you want with me first."

"*Muy razonable, Señor*," the man said, motioned for him to sit, and then waved off his soldiers for them to leave Marnoch with him. "What I want is to know about this Megalo*don*, eh?"

Well, Marnoch was the man to speak to, he supposed. "Okay. First I must ask you: Are you going to kill me and the others?"

"To be honest, *amigo*, I don't see any sense in that. If I kill another scientist–" Marnoch took note of 'another,' but held his tongue "–that could attract attention from your government. I assume you have many transponders aboard your ship and the submarine, *No es así?* Which means if you went missing for very long, they could find you?"

Marnoch held back from correcting the kingpin to use *boat* and *submersible*, instead replying, "That is true." He hadn't thought of that, but was damned glad this El Gato had.

"But for the second point, I need you alive to help me with the monster."

"Help you? How?"

"I'll just give it to you straight, my new friend. You know my name, *correcto?* You know who I am and what it is I do?"

Marnoch breathed in some courage, or possibly stupidity, and said, "Drugs. You smuggle drugs, obviously using this island in some way. Maybe storage? I don't know how any of that works. But what you do is drugs."

"*Exactamente.* I own two submarines, one which will be here shortly. But the other one is in the belly of the monster. I need to know some facts."

"All right, shoot." He swallowed. "I mean, ask away."

"What is it that happens to something that the monster eats? The stomach acid, will it digest metal? I ask because the submarine inside it is made of metal. And it is carrying more than a ton of my precious cocaine and methamphetamine. Will it poop it out or something? How long will that take? You see why I need an expert."

He saw, all right. "Sharks have the strongest stomach acid of any animal. The Megalodon is essentially a giant shark, so we can assume that it utilizes the same strength of acid, or even stronger."

Gato stroked his mustache for a moment and said, "So the sub?"

"Within twenty-four hours, the Meg's stomach will break it down. It will breach the hull and ..." Marnoch stopped as something hit him. "Did you say methamphetamines are on that sub?"

"Sí. Not as much as there is cocaine, but a good amount. Profitable as hell, you know, even more than coke in some ways."

Marnoch nodded and put up a single finger to let Gato know he was thinking. And thinking he was: Obviously, the meth he had found in the tissue of the Great White had somehow come from the swallowed submarine. But there had been no trace of cocaine. That meant the hull very likely had *not* been breached at the time of the crazy fish attack on Chris Newman's boat. For some reason, whoever was on that vessel had shoved a huge amount of drugs into the Meg's stomach. But why would they do that? Could they push out enough meth to make a difference?

"What I need to know, Mister Shark Scientist, is whether the monster will poop out my submarine. Or what about the acid in its stomach? What will happen to my drugs, eh?"

Marnoch let out a big breath. "Whew, well, you've got a lot of questions there, sir. But, let's see: No, it won't 'poop out' the submarine, actually *because* of the strength of the acid in its stomach. The hull will dissolve, perhaps over a week–we don't have any data on this, obviously–and so there won't be anything recognizable as a submarine being defecated."

"And the drugs?"

"If they're in the sub and the hull is breached, then it would enter … the Meg's bloodstream …" Lightning struck inside Marnoch's brain, recalling something very relevant, indeed. "Wait a second. One interesting feature of a shark's digestive system is that it can turn its stomach inside out and vomit out all the contents. This is usually done to scare away enemies, but it can also happen in response to toxicity in its system. I think your men shot out meth into the Meg's stomach in the hopes of making it vomit."

"How would they know this about sharks?"

"I doubt they do, but they're still trying to make it vomit them back into the water."

"*Increíble*," Gato said. "So we need to make the monster vomit, turn inside-out its weird stomach to get the sub and the tons of drugs back?"

"There are subtleties there, but essentially, yes."

"All right, wonderful, *maravilloso*." Gato nodded, looking around the desk perhaps for something to do with his hands, which right now were just being pressed together as he thought. "So, yes! How do we do this?"

"How do we do what?"

Gato blinked at him. "How do we get the sub back, eh? Get its stomach inside out?"

"Oh, wow, no, sorry. I don't think we have a way to induce it to vomit without some kind of threatening external stimulus. Of course, we must remember that if the Meg gets enough of your drugs it its system, it *will* vomit, but the cocaine will be irretrievably lost. For present-day sharks, you could have a bunch of orcas or a sperm whale to get it to make that kind of defensive maneuver, even other sharks if they were hungry enough." This seemed to make no difference whatsoever in Gato's expression. "But you have to understand, sir, the Megalodon is six or seven times as large as even the biggest Great White, and it has no natural predators from the present day. Not to be pessimistic, but you probably can't get the sub out without hurting the Meg."

Gato blinked at him again, this time with even greater incredulity. "I do not mean to offend you, *mi amigo*, but who gives a shit about a stupid shark when we are talking about ten million dollars?"

"What? The Megalodon is a unique animal–after the escape, the facility was barred from creating any more, although the belief is that there are as many as six pups out in the ocean near their parents."

"Let me ask you a question," Gato said, leaning back in his chair in what immediately struck Marnoch as anything but casual. "How many of the young *turistas* are on this island right now?"

"I have no way of knowing that."

"Give me your best guess, eh?"

Marnoch tried to remember if Chris Newman had given any suggestion at all of how many college kids and boat pilots there were for the weekend. Chris wasn't in charge of them all–that fell to the trip sponsor and organizer–but he had mentioned ten boats, and, assuming six people per boat … which who knew if that was an accurate estimate … he said, "Sixty or seventy, I think. But, if you don't mind my asking, why is that relevant?"

"Oh, you know," Gato said with even more feigned indifference, "I want to know how many people my soldiers need to kill to convince you to help with my recovery effort, *lo entiendes*?"

He understood indeed, and it made him feel like *his* stomach was going to turn inside out.

"Now, Doctor, what kind of weapons, fishing weapons, do these ten boats contain? There are, what, maybe hooks and harpoons and … how do you call them … spearguns?"

This made Marnoch instantly think of Chris shooting into the Meg's mouth, which the big shark definitely felt and changed course from eating the *Participant*. However, his poker face was practically nonexistent, and he saw the delight on El Gato's face from reading his own.

"*¡Maravillosas!* Maybe it is just wishful thinking, but I believe we do not have to kill your giant fish friend, if I can get your … cooperation."

Marnoch's heart jumped at the idea, because he knew El Gato wouldn't hesitate to kill the Meg if it meant getting his submarine–or what was left of it– and the drugs back. "How? What do you mean? I mean, yes, of course, but how?"

"You say that if we scare the monster enough, it will, em, *vomitar* its stomach contents, eh?" At

Marnoch's nod, he continued, "Then we need to scare the thing enough to make it sick."

El Gato asking how many people, how many boats, and what offensive weapons those boats might have onboard suddenly all snapped into place. Wishing beyond hope that he was wrong, Marnoch said, "You want to use the boats to scare the Megalodon."

"Kill it if that does not work, *sí*, but I don't care to kill the thing," El Gato said. "If you do not want to use the boats and the stupid children on the island, I have another submarine armed with a torpedo. We can just kill it."

Jesus! "I don't–that is, I highly doubt that would get you your drugs back, sir. It would kill the Meg, for sure, but then it would sink to the bottom and its stomach acid would still stay strong enough to breach the hull of your lost sub. Actually, the explosion would probably destroy the sub but possibly only injure the Megalodon. They are tough beings." He couldn't contain his admiration for the creatures.

El Gato chewed on this for a moment, then said, "Thank you for that information*, amigo*. Then we will not kill the thing. We will enlist the aid of the boats on the island. And the people, of course. Let us put all of them on the boats, leaving no one behind on shore."

"What? Why?"

"Let us say it will be *muy motivador*, eh?" El Gato said, then called to his soldier, "Bring all the men and march our scientist friend to the other side of the island, double-time. And when you get there, make sure the children and the others see the guns, *claro*?"

"Are you not coming, *jefe*?" the soldier said, perhaps unwisely.

But El Gato was all right. "I will take the cMarnoch. Now *vamos*."

***

"Davi?" Pedro said into the radio, but again, there was no reply. He was following the Megalodon by the tracker he had shot into it, so he knew where the sub must be, since it was inside it. The thing definitely swallowed it, and with it millions upon millions of dollars in product. He had no idea how long it took a giant dinosaur–or a regular shark, for that matter–to poop out something inedible that it had eaten, but he was going to follow this thing until it did.

The *Segunda* had caught up with the *Flotadora* now, but it held back in case the Meg was still in a sub-slurping mood. It had live torpedoes, but could they shoot and blow it up without destroying the *Buceadora*? They were as good as dead if they destroyed the massive shipment, Gato's most qualified mariners or not.

He watched the tracker signal, his eyes rarely leaving the instruments, when something very strange happened: a huge yellow blob entered into the sonar field. It was truly massive, Pedro saw, directly beneath his boat and just below and a few meters to port of the *Segunda*.

He was utterly perplexed. The thing was as big as the monster they were tracking. It was almost exactly the size of …of …

… *of a Megalodon.*

"O cristo protégeme," he said by way of an impromptu prayer for protection as the sonar indicated the Meg rising to meet the sub, which was smaller than the *Buceadora* and probably made for more of a snack than a full meal.

It was the mate. The giant thing had a mate, and she was here. Or maybe it was the him. It didn't matter. But this Megalodon was about to do to the second sub what the first Meg had done to the first sub. And that would be another $20 million gone in the blink of an eye. And poor Estaban on board, of course. But still, all that money.

Pedro hit the radio hard: "*¡Segunda!* Come in, Estaban!"

The response came almost immediately as the captain of the sub, Estaban, screamed into the radio, "*¡Ayúdame!* The thing is opening its mouth! *Help me!*"

And that was that. The radio went silent, the VHF waves unable to penetrate the body of the creature. Anyway, it didn't matter. They now had two poops to wait for.

He watched the second Meg move outside his radar's scope as it caught up with its mate. It acted like it had taken a mere sip of water, not like it had just ingested an entire metal submarine.

Estaban sounded like he was absolutely panicking, which hell, Pedro thought, he himself would probably be doing even worse. Especially as there was room for only one passenger on the *Segunda* with the amount of cocaine it was carrying. The space so tight and the comm being dead and … he had to force himself to breathe. He was never so glad not to be someone else in his life, and he had seen Gato have some pretty gruesome things done to people right in front of him.

Actually, sometimes he had been the one doing the horrible things. But he had never felt such stark relief as he did right now that he wasn't on the *Segundo*.

He took another breath. The island was very close, within sight. The Meg seemed almost to be just hanging out, and now, with its mate, maybe they were looking for a safe place to get their party started, as the Americans liked to say. He hoped the first Meg at least needed to make a nice *caca* before making love to its lady. Or whichever sex was which. He needed that cocaine out of those monsters, whatever it took.

The VHF crackled and then Gato's voice said simply, "Pedro."

Oh, no. Reluctantly, he picked up the handset. "Go for Pedro, *jefe*."

"You have the monster in sight? You are near the island?"

"*Sí*," Pedro said, his bones starting to shake at the thought of telling Gato what had just happened right underneath him. "*Y si*."

"*Excelente*. You must contact the *Segunda* and dock the *Flotadora* at the marina. It is time to–"

"*Jefe*, excuse me for interrupting, but there is important news."

Gato definitely sounded nonplussed as he said, "All right, Pedro. What is so urgent?"

Pedro told Gato everything about tracking the first Megalodon, then spotting its mate, then watching as the second Meg swallowed Gato's other submarine.

There was no reaction from Gato for a moment, and then he said icily, "Dock the boat."

Pedro didn't know why he was being blamed for the loss of the *Segunda*, but he had been with Gato long enough to know that he definitely was being blamed. "Pedro out," he said, and wished he really was.

***

Davi and Manny worked as a team like they never had before, even operating the sub, Manny grabbing a package of coke and slicing it open, then Davi taking it carefully from him, loading it into the decompression chamber until there was a man-sized pile of bags with precious drugs spilling out of them, then flooding the chamber and shooting the coke right into the creature's stomach.

The vessel's tiny windows showed the lights of the *Buceadora* illuminating a slimy environment with pieces of recently ingested fish and sharks and random-looking dead things along with bits of boat and other inorganic who knew what.

But after an hour or so of shoving the cocaine out into the thing's stomach, the light reflected back–which was getting noticeably dimmer the longer they didn't have moving seawater to charge the sub's batteries–had a definite diffused look, no doubt because it was getting absolutely buried with white powder.

After half an hour or so, they had unloaded at least half of the coke and all of the meth out into the monster when they felt the sub lurch, followed immediately by a deep gurgle that sounded to Davi exactly like what he thought the inside of a person would sound like when they were getting ready to throw up.

"*Continuemos*," Davi said, and put his hands out for Manny to fill with another two-kilo package. "It's working. Keep going."

They kept going, dumping a literal ton of cocaine into the Meg's stomach, and the lurching increased in power, making the men hold on in order not to fall over, and the awful gurgling increased in volume. It wouldn't be long now.

***

Aboard the other sub, the *Segunda*, Estaban was freaking out. How could a *Megalodon*, the most giant shark thing that ever lived, *sneak up* on a sub and swallow it without any warning? What the hell was goddamn Pedro *doing* up there?!? There was no way to know now, no way to contact him or anyone else on the radio or VHF, no way to know where he was, nothing to do but wait for a horrible death inside the creature.

Dios mío, the walls were closing in. Being inside a beast that could kill you was far worse than being surrounded simply by water pressure that could kill you. In this scenario, he was helpless, trapped, barely able to move … he could feel the panic rising in his chest.

He tried some breathing exercises all submariners were taught to deal with feelings of being trapped or alone physically or existentially, or both. He reminded himself again and again that nothing could eat a *submarine* and live to tell the tale. And he went to his happy place, a safe haven in his mind, a technique he had learned from his therapist during EMDR counseling. He pictured himself in a field of sunflowers, in the warm sunshine, in the open air, breathing it in, free as free could be.

But not for more than a moment. He was too freaked out; none of it worked. He was panicking, losing it, and recognizing that made him panic all the more. Then his gaze fell onto a lever and a button.

The torpedo.

The *Segunda* was never fully decommissioned because of the way that El Gato had acquired it from a bribed official with the Mexican Navy. It was on the way to be disarmed and do the rest of the decommissioning process when, what do you know, it "disappeared."

When El Gato got hold of the sub, he inherited with it a single torpedo already loaded in one of the tubes. Estaban had served on subs in the Mexican Navy, and he knew exactly how to fire one starting from zero, by himself. They had never tested this system in the *Segunda*–they only had the one torpedo, and even the Mexican government wasn't going to sell him any more–but the system worked exactly the same as on the larger sub he had served on, he was sure. Pretty sure, anyway.

He breathed *very* slightly easier. He could do something about his situation. He was empowered!

He had no idea which way was fore and which aft inside the Meg, but he didn't know if that really made much difference: he could blow the face off, or maybe blast through the tail, or just blowing through the side would be all the same with him.

He was going to escape! Without taking time to chicken out, Estaban pulled the lever and locked it into place, then pressed hard on the big red button.

And the untested torpedo immediately exploded inside its tube, blasting the *Segunda* into a million pieces and forcing the contents of one thousand bags of cocaine against the torn walls of the still-living Meg's stomach and directly into its bloodstream.

***

Chris froze in place as he saw Marnoch, Greene, Heyser, and the extremely traumatized-looking Jamie Cant marching in front of eight soldiers with AK-47s in hand just waiting to shoot anyone who stepped out of line.

At least they didn't kill them, Chris thought, and an unhelpful part of his brain added, *Not yet, anyway*.

The college kids started shouting in terror, and Chris was never so glad that these guys' girlfriends didn't usually come with them—the sound of panicked women screaming would probably be too much for him to handle without starting to scream himself.

The soldiers herded the fifty or so twenty-somethings toward the marina and started ordering them onto the boats, randomly but evenly distributed. Then the one who seemed to be in charge put Heyser on one boat, Greene on the next, then Andrzej, then motioned for Marnoch to get on the next boat and Chris on the one after. The poor kid, Jamie, stood behind Chris, not having been commanded to go to a boat yet and not about to ask for one, that was for sure.

"That won't work," Marnoch said, which shocked the hell out of Chris. "I'm not a boat captain. I'm a scientist. I need Mister Newman here to operate the vessel, *comprendes?*"

The soldiers looked at one another, the one in charge breaking it down into Spanish for his comrades. He stepped forward to tell Marnoch and Chris what was what, when the *chop-chop-chop* of El Gato's helicopter became too loud to ignore.

It set down on the beach, and Gato stepped out and leaned forward, exiting the airship before the rotors had even slowed down. He walked up to Chris and said, "You are the fisherman?"

My reputation precedes me, Chris thought. "You are the kingpin?"

"Ha! *Muy bueno*. Did Doctor Marnoch tell you what is to take place now, Mister Fisherman?"

"We haven't had the chance to discuss, what with your goons forcing everybody onto boats and everything." He was scared as hell, of course, but something about El Gato was so officious, he couldn't help but trying to resist the guy. Probably not the smartest move, but he maybe wasn't the smartest guy.

By chance and definitely by luck, Marnoch and Chris got the *Participant*, which really was Andrzej's tub, but it was good for the kids on that other boat that they had him at the wheel. Chris realized that the actual skippers of those vessels must have been so drunk back on shore that *armed militia* didn't wake them up enough to come out of their huts. He kind of wished he had been drunk enough, but he didn't do that when he had an actual fishing excursion; he'd had quite enough of doing his job under the influence.

"You, Mister Fisherman, you come here," Gato ordered before he could board the *Participant*. When Chris got there, Gato said, "What kinds of weapons do these boats have on board?"

"Weapons? Like guns?"

"No, *Señor*, I have plenty of guns. No, I mean like *arpones* ... what do you call them ..., *harpoons*. And spears or big metal hooks or whatever fishermen use."

"Rod and reel, mostly."

"No, no, we need to anger the Megalodon, even frighten it–"

"*Whoa* there, sir. You want to attack the *Megalodon* using five boats, one of which isn't even for fishing?" He realized that although the *Participant* wasn't a fishing boat, it probably had more defensive 'weapons' than even a fishing boat like *Killer Whale* had. "Did you hear what it did to my boat?"

"There is time for funny stories later, *Señor*. Before we get onto the water, I want you to get out everything that can hurt this giant shark. You have flare guns," Gato said, and this made Chris flinch at the memory of what Andrzej had to do to his tweaking brother, "you have sharp things to stab the monster. You have, what do you call them*, bang sticks, sí?* Whatever you think, but there better be a lot of it. We need to mess up that thing and make it throw up my drugs."

"Your … your *drugs?* Why does the Meg have your drugs?"

Marnoch stepped up. "I'll explain everything on the boat. Let's just do what he says."

The radio at his primary soldier's hip crackled and a voice came through: "El Gato? *Jefe*, please respond."

The kingpin looked annoyed as he took the radio from the soldier and said, "Copy you, Pedro. What is it? Where are you?"

"I'm coming around the south of the island toward the tourist side, *jefe*. I'm right behind the Megalodons."

"Megalo*dons?* Plural?"

"*Sí.* The *Buceadora* is inside one and the *Segunda* is inside the other. Do you see the monsters? They are very close to the surface, and the water here is not so deep."

Gato put out his hand and one of the soldier detail seemed to have gleaned from the conversation that he was to place binoculars in it. Which he did and immediately scanned the water to the south and …

"Yes. There they are," Gato said, and Chris squinted. He could see, even without binoculars, dark shapes under the water, immense shadows. He looked at Marnoch, who obviously saw the same. But on Marnoch's face wasn't fear or dread, instead almost a joy. It made sense–these were, after all, what the man's entire career was based on, Chris knew.

Then Marnoch's expression lost its joy and changed to quizzical, then to realization, then to a different kind of fear than what Chris–and, he would be willing to bet, just about everyone on any of the boats–was feeling.

"Marnoch? What's going on? What are you seeing?"

Marnoch shook his head. "I don't exactly know. But … their snouts keep rising out of the water. That's very unusual, at least based on my experience around them. And look, they're actually rocking back and forth, both of them. See how the pectoral fins rise out of the water, first on one side and then on the other?"

Chris did see. "It's like they're flopping around. Like they have excess … oh, shit."

"Yeah. Like they have excess energy." He leaned in close to Chris and said as quietly as he possibly could, "Like they have a massive amount of stimulant in their systems."

"It's too late," Chris whispered even quieter than Marnoch had. "The drugs are lost–they're in the Megalodon now. Those things are *high as hell*. And I've heard about El Gato. The news says he's murdered entire villages when in a rage."

"We can't let him know, 'cause he'll kill us. But we can't go out there. Those things are going to go *crazy*."

"Hey, what are you saying to each other?" Gato said sharply. "Get on your boats and let us go make this thing sick, eh? If we don't, Mister Fisherman and Doctor Scientist ... well, no need for unpleasantness. Let's just do it and get me my cocaine, *entendio?* Then we can all stay friends."

Chris nodded along with Marnoch, but as they walked down the dock to the *Participant*, he said, "We can't let these kids go out there and get killed. Look." He pointed at the two giant creatures, which were starting to kind of bob their mouths, then their tails, above the waves.

They could see Pedro's boat now, following the leviathans. It was keeping a safe distance (whatever that meant in this situation), but the water around it was getting choppy thanks to the sometimes rhythmic, sometimes erratic, motion of the giant creatures.

But El Gato had obviously noticed the same thing, and he put the binoculars up to his eyes again. "Doctor Marnoch, what is happening there? Why are the monsters moving like that?"

Chris's eyes went wide. Surely Marnoch wasn't going to tell this murderous drug smuggler that millions upon millions' worth of his profit had just been consumed, that the things were starting to feel the effects of a submarine each packed to the gills with cocaine absorbed into their systems. No, he would opt for dishonesty and momentary safety.

"They are starting their mating ritual," Marnoch said. "This might be the perfect time to send out the *Participant*, my boat, since it has all the weapons on it. *So* many weapons."

"Yes, your boat and the other boats. The more, the merrier, eh?"

"Actually, what I was thinking was that it would be more effective–"

"*María, madre de dios!*" Gato cried. "No, no no *no!*"

Chris's gaze shot to where the Megs and the boat were, and he could see that both of the Megs were rearing up out of the water, thrashing violently and sending off huge waves from moving such huge bodies in such relatively shallow water. And one of them came up from under Pedro's boat and launched it into the air. When it hit the water again, it was in pieces.

Taking advantage of Gato staring in disbelief through the binoculars, Chris started making his way backwards toward the *Participant*, motioning for Marnoch to follow. When Marnoch caught up to him, also walking backwards as casually as possible, Chris said in a low voice, "Get in the boat. We're taking off."

"*With the Megs going crazy?*" Marnoch whispered as loudly as could still be considered whispering. "If they get to us, we're dead."

"Yeah, well, we're dead if we stay here," Chris said, now watching Gato practically jumping up and down in rage. He had his VHF receiver out and was screaming into it, "*Pedro! Come in or I will chop you into dog meat! RESPÓNDEME, PEDRO!*"

"Fair enough," Marnoch said, and they very quietly boarded the *Participant*. The soldiers were watching them, but it seemed they thought that the people were supposed to be getting on the boats, something for which Chris was grateful, indeed.

Chris signaled to the other sailors for them to take the boats out and sail around the island opposite to the direction where the Megs were now devouring the remains of Gato's boat along with its sailors, he assumed. *Poor bastard.*

The boats started up, and immediately Chris heard exactly what he was dreading: Gato shouting at them and ordering for them to return, Chris guessed because he really did want to murder every one of them to burn off some of his energy. But the boats were each now ten or twenty feet from the dock and moving away with increasing speed under motor power..

One of the soldiers raised his machine gun, but Gato waved him off, instead–Chris could see even from this distance–smiling at something in his head so dark, Chris didn't even want to know what it was.

Although he did know, he was sure. That look was El Gato the sadistic kingpin watching five boats of people leaving the dock to their certain doom, to their certain to be painful and terrifying doom.

Chris manned the controls, taking the *Participant* on its arc around the island with the other boats when he heard a roar mixed with a shriek mixed with ten thousand gallons of water being violently displaced behind him. He turned and saw that one of the Megs was now thrashing and jumping and–

–and, Jesus, erupting into an explosion of blood coming from its mouth, its eyes, its nostrils, everything. Blood vented from everywhere at once, and after a few more epic spasms, it fell quiet, rocking back and forth in its own red waves.

Shouts and the sounds of puking came from the boats as the men on them saw the gory catastrophe.

"Marnoch," Chris said.

"I see it."

"Did something explode inside it? What the hell just happened?"

"I don't know, but it seemed to suffer massive hemorrhaging. An interior explosion from what, a torpedo? Do these subs have that kind of armament? But this looks like its insides were just shredded and everything collapsed in a massive coke-fueled eruption. We just watched a Megalodon OD on drugs going straight into its bloodstream."

"Holy mother of God," Chris said, then noticed what the other Meg was doing. "Is that one … is it *eating* the other one?"

He looked over and saw Marnoch had a huge pair of binoculars already out. "Um … yeah. And guess what else?"

"Jesus, what else could there be?"

"The pups," Marnoch said, sounding horrified and fascinated in equal measure. "Oh, man … the pups are there … and they're eating it, too."

"That can't be good."

"The pups are smaller, and they and the surviving Meg are now ingesting cocaine-drenched blood and tissue of its mate. We've got about five minutes, and then all hell is going to break loose."

Chris nodded; he had already figured as much.

***

If El Gato had carried a weapon instead of leaving them to his stooges, he probably would have lit up every one of those stupid *gringo* boats just out of sheer fury, adding their blood to the blood of the giant monster out there. This one disaster alone would put his operation far behind Jalisco, both of his submarines gone, his command ship gone, and *forty goddamn million dollars* of cocaine and meth gone, fed to the fishes.

"What orders, *jefe?*" his commander asked. He was following the boats going around the island with his eyes. Gato couldn't tell if the man's finger was literally itching on the trigger of his weapon, but he did seem like a snake coiled to strike at the smallest invitation from his boss.

He wanted them to kill everyone, set the boats aflame, and drop bombs onto those *maldito* dinosaur sharks, which weren't even supposed to *exist*. Then he wanted to take the soldiers' machine guns and kill them as well, then get in the helicopter back to Tijuana and kill the first people he saw.

He watched the boats moving almost out of sight. Then he looked back at the red foam of the Megalodon frenzy not half a mile away. He then returned his gaze to the boats.

Gato smiled and indicated the machine gun. "Do not let those boats come back to shore. Do what you have to in order to persuade them to stay at sea, eh?" His smile wasn't that of a cat at that moment … no, his eyes and mouth were more like that of a shark: cold as hell. "The monsters and its babies will see them soon, and then they can go the way of my cocaine. And then we go up and shoot the giant *puta* until it dies. You can shoot anything to death, if you have enough ammo to spare. Do we have enough to spare, *amigo?*"

"*Sí, jefe,*" the soldier said, and very nearly smiled.

***

"They're not going to let us dock," Chris said to Marnoch as they watched the heavily armed soldiers walking the perimeter of the island, keeping them in sight, and that meant them in sight of their machine guns. The other boats followed, staying far enough away from the shallows not to run themselves aground but not so far that it was deep enough for the Megalodons to reach them. They were following Chris and Marnoch's moves in the *Participant*. He added, "We shouldn't even try."

"I can't see the Meg and its pups," Marnoch said, looking panicked for the first time Chris had seen.

"Sorry, but what does that matter?"

"We're going to be the most noticeable moving things near them. In their heightened state, if they see us, they're coming after us."

"*They?* That one Meg is definitely dead."

"The pups, Chris. The last we saw, they're consuming the blood of their parent. They're a lot smaller than a full-grown Megalodon, which means the effect on them will be outsize." At the sound of his own words, Marnoch looked like he was going to freeze up entirely. Chris hoped he wouldn't have to slap him or something to bring him back. "In other words, we're between a rock and a hard place. We can't land our boats or those guys will shoot to kill all of us. But as soon as we come out on the other side of the island, the Megs will see us, and even one of those pups could take us out by itself if it really wanted to right now."

"Certain death or probable death. I guess we have to go for probable."

Marnoch nodded weakly.

"But don't forget, these are essentially just ginormous fish. And you have a secret weapon."

"What do you mean?"

"You've got *The Fishing Guy!*" Chris said, and thought he saw a glimmer of hope in Marnoch's eyes, or maybe it was fear, or maybe it was incredulity. Maybe all three. He made sure Marnoch was present and listening as he added, "We've got ten minutes until we get back. Show me what you've got on the boat, and let's get fishing."

***

Davi and Manny aboard the *Buceadora* inside the monster were rocked by the shock wave in the water that shot across the beast's belly pushing them one way, striking the wall of the stomach, and being swept back as the water came back. "It's working!" Davi said with intense excitement and not a little relief.

Manny had come down from the meth now, and Davi could see the man was actually crying from the drugs and the horror and now the break in the clouds.

"It's puking, I think. The water is being forced out, it feels like. We're going to be in the next wave, *amigo*. Get yourself ready!"

This was it. *They were going to make it!* Just as they braced themselves to be rocketing out of the thing's system, an alarm sounded from the instrument panel.

The hull! It was starting to–

The hull gave way and the submarine imploded. A few seconds later, the Megalodon vomited the crushed remnants out into the ocean.

***

The *Participant* and the boats following it were moving too fast to make a U-turn, and the paramilitary soldiers probably would have put a stop to that anyway, Chris thought. So it was time to go fishing. The boat had a large net, flare guns, spearguns and spears, even a harpoon, although it was hard for Chris to think about what a research vessel was doing with one of those.

Since all of the boats had their radios destroyed, Chris couldn't send instructions to them that way about the fishing gear. But there were semaphore flags on the boat, which meant that someone there knew how to use them.

"Marnoch," he said. "Does your crew know semaphore?"

"Yes, of course. We're an international res–"

"Great. I need you to send a message to your crew on the other boats."

Chris gave him the message, and Marnoch duly signaled the other boats:

R-E-A-D-Y-N-E-T-S-F-L-A-R-E-G-U-N-S-H-A-R-P-O-O-N-S

He could only hope that the others would understand why, although he really couldn't tell why they wouldn't. There wasn't anything to do but face the Megs. *Probable death versus definite death*, he reminded himself.

They finally came around to the west-facing side of the island, the smugglers' side. And there they were, thrashing in the water, closer now, torn pieces of smaller sharks and fish being launched into wide arcs by the fury of the agitated Megalodons.

Then, all of a sudden, they stopped.

Chris's blood turned cold.

"They see us," Marnoch said.

"We're still shallow enough that they can't reach us," Chris said, and hoped he was right. The way the Meg and its young had been writhing and flopping and devouring and ripping apart the other fish, it would be game over pretty fast. "But we're gonna have to get out of here."

This El Gato was a real asshole. He wanted them all to die just because he wanted to punish them for something they had nothing to do with at all except being in the wrong place at the wrong time. And, with armed soldiers obviously ready to shoot if they got too close to shore and murderous sea monsters ready to eat them if they got too far away, it looked like the drug kingpin would get his wish.

There was one way out, however: if they sailed away from the island on a tack that kept the island itself and the Megalodons in a line so the island shielded them from view, then they could go out onto the open sea, hopefully long enough to wait out the Megs' drug-fueled frenzy.

More semaphore to the other boats:

F-O-L-L-O-W-M-E-S-T-A-Y-I-N-L-I-N-E

Cutting the motor to almost nothing to avoid noise that might attract attention from the creatures, Chris pulled away from the island in the opposite direction from them, motioning for them to follow as instructed by the semaphore message. And they did.

"How far do you think we need to go until it's safe?" Chris asked Marnoch.

"How far can you get?" Marnoch said wryly, then worked out something in his head. "I think if we can get two miles away, we can make a break for the mainland. We're going, what, two knots?"

"Just about."

"Then we have an hour; we have to just kind of putter along. But we can make it, Skipper! Nice job!"

Chris didn't know about that, but it did feel good to do *something* about the situation.

Slowly, so slowly, the island shrank behind them.

***

El Gato did not like to be questioned. That's why he shot one of the soldiers right in front of the rest. That definitely got their attention.

Actually, the question wasn't even a question. It was the soldier looking out at the boats inching away from the island and saying, "*Jefe*, they are escaping."

"Nobody escapes from El Gato," he said with pride, and shot the soldier in the belly, which meant the man would die slowly and agonizingly, a warning to anyone else who didn't believe El Gato was the *grande jefe* in the drug trade. No *estúpido pez gigante*, no *estúpido pescador*, no *estúpido científico* was going to make *him* look stupid. If Jalisco could not defeat him, then no stupid fish or fisherman or scientist was going to.

"Radio the pilot," he said to the next soldier in line. "Get the helicopter over here, and make sure your weapons are ready. We are going fishing for the fisherman, eh?"

It wasn't a particularly funny comment, but everyone made sure to laugh.

***

"I want you to know I never doubted you, Chris," Marnoch said, almost overwhelmed by relief. "But to see it working, my God."

Chris kept looking behind them to make sure everyone was in tandem in the straight line. Marnoch had helped him with keeping on the right heading, which was almost precisely west-northwest. He watched the compass, and Chris watched the boats behind them.

It was working. In less than half an hour, they would be safely … safely …

Uh oh.

El Gato's black military helicopter was taking off from the island and immediately nosed forward and headed towards them. It quickly overtook the line and hovered just in front of the *Participant* so the boat could not continue forward without approaching it even closer, which was something Chris most certainly did not want to do.

From a megaphone, Gato said with slight amusement in his voice, "Turn around, Doctor Marnoch. You are not getting away from me and the Megalogon."

MegaloDON, Marnoch's mind automatically corrected, but he thought he might just keep that to himself. He looked at Chris, who seemed as perplexed as Marnoch did.

"What do we do?" Chris asked plainly. This was making it clear that Chris was only a sailor and Marnoch was the Megalodon expert. Only he would know what to do if they couldn't go forward and had to get within view of the insane giant creatures.

"We–" Marnoch started, but was cut off by the loudest gunfire he could have imagined, a sudden *pop-pop-pop* that made his ears ring and his heart almost beat out of his chest.

"Aw, Christ!" Chris shouted in horror and dismay as they watched the last ship in line-the one with Heyser aboard as captain-fly into bits of fiberglass and wood, the ten people aboard reduced to shreds by the machine gun fire from three soldiers in the helicopter. The ship didn't sink, but it did start floating sideways, instantly derelict. Everyone was dead.

"Turn around, Doctor Marnoch."

Although the order was directed towards Marnoch, Chris immediately leaned on the wheel and turned up the throttle, making an intentionally showy arc that quickly pointed him back towards the island. Actually, not directly back, Marnoch saw, as Chris had obviously surmised that getting back on that straight line between them and the Megs with the island still blocking them might make the bastard on the helicopter even madder. The other boats all turned from where they were as well, a synchronized move that probably looked pretty impressive from the helicopter.

"Very good!" came the voice from the megaphone, just audible over the cMarnoch blades. "Now, you know where to go."

Chris looked at Marnoch, and Marnoch knew what he was thinking: *Get the gear*. The only chance against the raving Megalodon and its offspring that were bigger than Great Whites was to attack, as futile as that had to be.

The cMarnoch still hovered heavily in the air, making sure all the boats were heading the right way. Marnoch wanted to semaphore instructions to the others about using anything they had on board. The last option was to ram the thing with a boat, but he couldn't see how that would make any difference at all except getting everyone on the boat killed and annoying the Megalodon even more. To do that, it would have to be one killing blow.

As they got closer to the Megs, Marnoch could see that fish of all sizes were swimming as fast as possible from the maddened leviathans. The ocean itself seemed to have a blood-red tint which got darker the closer they got.

"What the heck is he doing?" Marnoch asked Chris as the boat with Greene on it, the stupid asshole from AIMS Queensland at the helm, rushed past them towards the violent thrashing that was now only about a quarter mile away, the idiot yelling at the top of his lungs some kind of wild war cry, while the others on the boat were just screaming for him to stop. But he could fight them off with one arm, it seemed, and it was probably too late anyway, the momentum of the speeding craft too much to change tack fast enough now.

Marnoch didn't know what Greene's plan was, if he even had one, but whatever it was ended as the Meg seemed to sense it to its portside and swung its enormous body towards Greene's boat, twisting almost out of the water, and bringing its thrashing body directly down on them. The resultant splash and wave flew out like the Megalodon was cannonballing at a city pool. He couldn't even see anything of Greene's boat, it had been crushed so quickly and destroyed so completely.

Now the Meg was pointed towards the *Participant* and the other two remaining boats. Its pups were making the water white all around their parent, and that, it seemed, was keeping the creature from spotting them. That wouldn't last, however; sooner rather than later, the Meg would see them and come for them.

"I wish we had a torpedo, take that thing down," Chris said, then immediately added to the scientist who had devoted his career to studying *that thing*: "Sorry."

"Don't be," Marnoch said. "Screw that druggie bastard."

They shared a gallows chuckle at that, but after a moment Marnoch realized they *did* have a torpedo. Well, something that could be used as one, anyway.

The submersible on board, the *Sinker*. It was hollow, of course, and could be filled with the ethanol-gasoline mixture that fueled the *Participant*, and it could be controlled remotely, being a submersible and not a submarine.

"What's our fuel like?"

"What?" Chris snapped. "It's good, we have plenty of fuel, okay? What the hell does that matter?"

"Oh, it matters."

***

El Gato was satisfied with his plan. Well, it wasn't a *plan* exactly, but he did want to see the *gringos* die right in front of him and get some tiny enjoyment, at least, after losing a fortune in cocaine and meth. He was riding the high of cruelty and murder–he could deal with the financial garbage when he returned to Tijuana. All the screaming and dying would provide a little comfort in this difficult time.

The remaining boats were near the beast now, that one *idiota* charging the thing and being smashed into pieces and the bodies broken for the young to snatch up and swallow. It was a bloodbath, but not as bad as it would get, if Gato had his way. And he would have his way, goddamnit.

He had the pilot take the cMarnoch closer to the crazed Megalodon, a giant shark–massive and gray surrounded by whitewater suffused with red, now a maniac monster. The *swoosh* created by the wide sweep of its tail was almost otherworldly in the sound it made, somewhere between a roaring jet engine and a crashing tidal wave.

And he … wait … *What the hell is that?*

It was the little submarine from the research boat with Doctor Marnoch and the fisherman. It was close enough to the surface to see from the helicopter, but getting so close to the monsters and its spawn that it was going to be lost to the surf in a matter of moments. It wasn't too deep not to be visible from above, but it was deep enough that it would be a challenge to shoot straight and hit it.

Were they trying to ram the thing? If they thought he was going to let them off that easy–what if it worked and the creature calmed down? That would mean they would have relief before he ended their lives with machine guns pointed at them and firing. No, it was unacceptable that they would die quickly, thinking until that moment that they had defeated the beast.

There was no way he was letting that happen. He would not let them die happy.

"Get in close on that submarine," he told the pilot. "You're gonna have to get near the surface for the bullets to puncture it."

But the pilot said, "*Jefe*, we cannot get too close to the Megalodon. The little ones have gone away– maybe they did not have so much of the drugs in their bodies? But the big one, the giant–we cannot get too close."

Gato fumed. "We can get as close as I *say* we can get, *amigo*. Now get down there before I decide to do something very bad to your family, eh?"

The pilot didn't even respond to that, instead just putting the copter's nose down and throttling to move them in. They were so close now that some seafoam dotted the windscreen.

Gato shouted to the *puta* soldiers who looked absolutely terrified being this close to the creature, "Shoot the sub! *Shoot the sub! KILL THEM!*"

One thing Gato loved about his underlings was that they knew to do what he told them, unless they no longer were so attached to their lives.

They shot at the *Sinker*, some bullets being deflected from their entry into the water. But one finally struck true, and the sons of bitches who thought they were going to win by sacrificing just one of their own instead of everyone were about to be sorely disapp–

The submersible exploded, hurling a shock wave of water into the air and into the rotors of the Mi-8MT formerly armed gunship, which failed almost immediately and sent the helicopter crashing into the water … but they hadn't been high enough to make the fall fatal.

No, they crashed right next to the tweaking Megalodon, and the last thing El Gato saw was the monster opening its jaws to crush them, and the last thing he heard was his own scream.

***

Chris saw that the explosion next to the Meg did the huge animal no damage, since the shock wave from the exploding fuel-filled submersible caught the creature mid-thrash in the opposite direction, and the helicopter crashed into the water right in front of its mouth. And finally, the copter and its passengers were crushed between the Megalodon's epic jaws. It was busy for the moment, and that moment was time to get the hell away from it while it was distracted.

He wasted no time in turning and shouting at the remaining three boats to head for the island as fast as they could. The creature seemed nowhere near done with its drug-fueled freakout, so the island was the only safe place until it rode it out and swam away, probably itself wondering what the hell just happened.

As he turned the boat towards Persuasion Island, he smiled and said to Marnoch, "Good thinking with the sub, man. You made El Gato shoot and blow it up and frickin' take himself out in the process. *Bravo*."

Marnoch grimaced and laughed, the remote control for the *Sinker* still in his hand. "Actually, I thought the Meg was going to bite down on it. I got lucky that El Gato couldn't resist."

"Luck beats skill every time."

From behind them came the words, "Yeah … lucky …" It was a pale and shaking college kid, Jamie, who then fainted dead away.

THE END

Check out other great
Sea Monster Novels!

Robert J. Stava

NEPTUNES RECKONING

At the easternmost end of Long Island lies a seaside town known as Montauk. Ground Zero on the Eastern seaboard for all manner of conspiracy theories involving it's hidden Cold War military base, rumors of time-travel experiments and alien visitors... For renowned Naval historian William Vanek it's the where his grandfather's ship went down on a Top Secret mission during WWII code-named "Neptune's Reckoning". Together with Marine Biologist Daniel Cheung and disgraced French underwater explorer Arnaud Navarre, he's about to discover the truth behind the urban legends: a nightmare from beyond space and time that has been reawakened by global warming and toxic dumping, a nightmare the government tried to keep submerged. Neptune's Reckoning. Terror knows no depth

Bestselling collection

DEAD BAIT

A husband hell-bent on revenge hunts a Wereshark... A Russian mail order bride with a fishy secret... Crabs with a collective consciousness... A vampire who transforms into a Candiru... Zombie piranha...Bait that will have you crawling out of your skin and more. Drawing on horror, humor with a helping of dark fantasy and a touch of deviance, these 19 contemporary stories pay homage to the monsters that lurk in the murky waters of our imaginations. If you thought it was safe to go back in the water... Think Again!

Check out other great

Sea Monster Novels!

Matt James

SUB-ZERO

The only thing colder than the Antarctic air is the icy chill of death... Off the coast of McMurdo Station, in the frigid waters of the Southern Ocean, a new species of Antarctic octopus is unintentionally discovered. Specialists aboard a state-of-the-art DARPA research vessel aim to apply the animal's "sub-zero venom" to one of their projects: An experimental painkiller designed for soldiers on the front lines. All is going according to plan until the ship is caught in an intense storm. The retrofitted tanker is rocked, and the onboard laboratory is destroyed. Amid the chaos, the lead scientist is infected by a strange virus while conducting the specimen's dissection. The scientist didn't die in the accident. He changed.

Alister Hodge

THE CAVERN

When a sink hole opens up near the Australian outback town of Pintalba, it uncovers a pristine cave system. Sam joins an expedition to explore the subterranean passages as paramedic support, hoping to remain unneeded at base camp. But, when one of the cavers is injured, he must overcome paralysing claustrophobia to dive pitch-black waters and squeeze through the bowels of the earth. Soon he will find there are fates worse than being buried alive, for in the abandoned mines and caves beneath Pintalba, there are ravenous teeth in the dark. As a savage predator targets the group with hideous ferocity, Sam and his friends must fight for their lives if they are ever to see the sun again.

Check out other great

Sea Monster Novels!

Michael Cole

MEGALODON VS COLOSSAL SNAKE

Brought to life by the miracle of DNA cloning, a 93-foot Megalodon shark has escaped captivity. With an insatiable appetite and unmatched aggression, it travels west for the Georgia coast, leaving a path of destruction in its wake. Bullets and harpoons can't penetrate it, steel nets can't hold it, and it's only a matter of time before the whole world finds out about it. In a race to stop the beast, the organization responsible recruit a marine biologist and a herpetologist to develop a plan to catch it. To do it, they must unleash the company's other genetically modified experiment—a 150-foot snake, resurrected from the DNA of the mighty Titanoboa. The pursuit leads to inevitable combat, and the scientists are forced to witness the deadly realities of genetic tampering. As the battle escalates, it is clear nobody is safe...and that nature never intended for these beasts to return. As the destruction mounts, and the death toll climbs, the true loser of Megalodon vs. Colossal Snake is humanity.

Tim Waggoner

TEETH OF THE SEA

They glide through dark waters, sleek and silent as death itself. Ancient predators with only two desires – to feed and reproduce. They've traveled to the resort island of Las Dagas to do both, and the guests make tempting meals. The humans are on land, though, out of reach. But the resort's main feature is an intricate canal system . . . . . . and it's starting to rain.